A … Ops / Immortal Ops)

by

Mandy M. Roth

Act of Surrender (PSI-Ops / Immortal Ops) © Copyright 2014, Mandy M. Roth
First Electronic Printing September 2014, The Raven Books
Trade Paperback Printing September 2014
Cover art by Natalie Winters, © Copyright 2014
Edited by: Suz G.
Final Line Edits by: Dianne B.
PRINT ISBN-13: 978-1501039898
PRINT ISBN-10: 150103989X

This novel is a work of fiction and intended for mature audiences only. Any and all characters, names, events, places and incidents are used under the umbrella of fiction and are of the author's imagination and should not be confused with fact. Any resemblance to persons, living or dead, or events or places or locales is merely coincidence.

The Raven
Published by Raven Books
www.ravenhappyhour.com ~ www.theravenbooks.com

Mandy M. Roth Featured Books

Immortal Ops Series

Immortal Ops
Critical Intelligence
Radar Deception
Strategic Vulnerability
Tactical Magik
Administrative Control
Separation Zone
Area of Influence
Desired Perception
Carnal Diversions
Zone of Action

PSI-Ops Series (Part of the Immortal Ops World)

Act of Mercy
Act of Surrender
Act of Submission
Act of Security
Act of Command
Act of Passion
Act of Engagement
Act of Pride
Act of Duty

Immortal Outcasts (Part of the Immortal Ops World)

Broken Communication
Damage Report
Wrecked Intel
Isolated Maneuver
Intelligence Malfunction

Shadow Agents Series & Crimson Sentinels Series (Part of the Immortal Ops World) Coming Soon!

Act of Surrender (PSI-Ops Series / Immortal Ops)

Book Two in the PSI-Ops Series

Dr. James Hagen thought he'd bid Paranormal Security and Intelligence Agency good riddance nearly ten years back. He'd been an operative with them for so long that carving out a new path in life had taken time, but he'd achieved it. He'd made it his mission in life to help the wayward find a path again, to help those who couldn't help themselves. All that changed when he fell into enemy hands. Now, unable to fully heal and plagued by nightmares and choppy visions of what is to come, James isn't sure if he can keep going. That is, until he meets PSI's newest person of interest—a quirky, sexy cyberpunk who totally turns his world upside down.

Laney Steele knows she's onto something. It doesn't matter that most have written her off as a conspiracy theorist and a hacktivist. She knows the government is hiding the existence of super soldiers who can shapeshift into animals. She's so sure that she puts herself on the line to find out more, only what she uncovers isn't exactly what she was hoping for, and it has a heck of a lot more to do with her than she ever thought possible. When her newfound online gamer buddy turns out to be a super solider, she throws caution to the wind just for a chance to be with him. Neither one of them realize the enemy has been lurking, waiting for the perfect moment to strike—again.

Dedication

Thank you, readers, for sticking with me for over ten years on this wild ride. And, as always, thank you to the men and women who put their lives on the line for our freedom. Thank you for serving our country and for all you do, and thank you to their spouses, significant others and family members for all you do as well.

Praise for Mandy M. Roth's Immortal Ops World

Silver Star Award—*I feel Immortal Ops deserves a Silver Star Award as this book was so flawlessly written with elements of intrigue, suspense and some scorching hot scenes*—Aggie Tsirikas—Just Erotic Romance Reviews

5 Stars—*Immortal Ops is a fascinating short story. The characters just seem to jump out at you. Ms. Roth wrote the main and secondary characters with such depth of emotions and heartfelt compassion I found myself really caring for them*—Susan Holly—Just Erotic Romance Reviews

Immortal Ops packs the action of a Hollywood thriller with the smoldering heat that readers can expect from Ms. Roth. Put it on your hot list...and keep it there! —The Road to Romance

5 Stars—*Her characters are so realistic, I find myself wondering about the fine line between fact and fiction...This was one captivating tale that I did not want to end. Just the right touch of humor endeared these characters to me even more*—eCataRomance Reviews

5 Steamy Cups of Coffee—*Combining the world of secret government operations with mythical creatures as if they were*

an everyday thing, she (Ms. Roth) then has the audacity to make you actually believe it and wonder if there could be some truth to it. I know I did. Nora Roberts once told me that there are some people who are good writers and some who are good storytellers, but the best is a combination of both and I believe Ms. Roth is just that. Mandy Roth never fails to surpass herself—coffeetimeromance

Mandy Roth kicks ass in this story—inthelibraryreview

Immortal Ops Series and PSI-Ops Series Helper

(This will be updated in each upcoming book as new characters are introduced.)

Paranormal Security and Intelligence (PSI) Operatives

General Jack C. Newman: Director of Operations for PSI, werelion. Adoptive father of Missy Carter-Majors.

Duke Marlow: PSI-Operative, werewolf. Mated to Mercy. Book: Act of Mercy (PSI-Ops)

Doctor James (Jimmy) Hagen: PSI-Operative, werewolf. Took a ten-year hiatus from PSI. Book: Act of Surrender (PSI-Ops)

Striker (Dougal) McCracken: PSI-Operative, werewolf.

Miles (Boomer) Walsh: PSI-Operative, werepanther.

Captain Corbin Jones: Operations coordinator and captain for PSI-Ops Team Five, werelion.

Malik (Tut) Nasser: PSI-Operative, (PSI-Ops).

Colonel Ulric Lovett: Direction of Operations, PSI-London Division.

Immortal Ops (I-Ops) Team Members

Lukian Vlakhusha: Alpha-Dog-One. Team captain, werewolf, King of the Lycans, mated to Peren Matthews (Daughter of Dr. Lakeland Matthews). Book: Immortal Ops (Immortal Ops)

Geoffroi (Roi) Majors: Alpha-Dog-Two. Second in command, werewolf, blood-bound brother to Lukian, mated to Melissa "Missy" Carter-Majors. Book: Critical Intelligence (Immortal Ops)

Doctor Thaddeus Green: Bravo-Dog-One. Scientist, tech guru, werepanther, mated to Melanie Daly-Green (sister of Eadan Green). Book: Radar Deception (Immortal Ops)

Jonathon (Jon) Reynell: Bravo-Dog-Two. Sniper, weretiger. As of this book not currently mated. Book: Separation Zone (Immortal Ops)

Wilson Rousseau: Bravo-Dog-Three. Resident smart-ass, wererat, mated to Kimberly (Daughter of Culann of the Council) Book: Strategic Vulnerability (Immortal Ops)

Eadan Daly: Alpha-Dog-Three. PSI-Op and handler on loan to the I-Ops to round out the team, Fae, mated to Inara

Nash. Brother of Melanie Daly-Green. Book: Tactical Magik (Immortal Ops)

Colonel Asher Brooks: Chief of Operations and point person for the Immortal Ops Team. Mated to Jinx, magik, succubus, well-known, well-connected madam to the underground paranormal community. Book: Administrative Control (Immortal Ops)

Miscellaneous

Culann of the Council: Father to Kimberly (who is mated to Wilson). Badass Fae.

Pierre Molyneux: Master vampire bent on creating a race of super soldiers. Hides behind being a famous art dealer in order to launder money.

Gisbert Krauss: Mad scientist who wants to create a master race of supernaturals.

Walter Helmuth: Head of Seattle's paranormal underground. In league with Molyneux and Krauss.

Dr. Lakeland Matthews: Scientist, vital role in the creation of a successful Immortal Ops Team. Father to Peren Matthews.

Dr. Bertrand: Mad scientist with Donavon Dynamics Corporation (The Corporation).

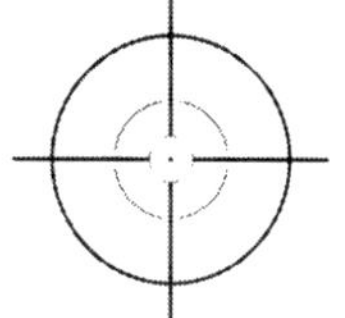

Chapter One

Paranormal Security and Intelligence Division B Headquarters, classified location…

Dr. James Hagen sat up fast, surprised he'd dozed off at his work station. It wasn't as if the lab area was exactly brimming over with comfort. There were counters, higher than average due to the fact most of the people who worked in the building were very tall. A row of stools, reinforced to withstand the weight of shifter males, dotted the area just beneath the counter. They were fairly plain—metal bottoms with black leather tops. Not to mention the counters themselves were stocked with various items of lab equipment.

James rubbed his forehead, pretty sure he had a mark from his head pressing against the centrifuge machine. As he felt it more, he realized the manufacturer's plate had left an impression as well. He'd have looked in a mirror had one been close. Best it wasn't. Seeing himself with letters in his forehead wouldn't do anything to help his mood. The indents would thankfully go away within a minute or two. He didn't want to explain it to his fellow teammates. They'd tease him about it for weeks.

Maybe more.

His office, which was off the main lab and clinic area, was much more conducive to resting. It had an oversized, expensive, leather sofa in it along with a huge desk, state-of the-art computers, and even high-end artwork on the walls. The people in charge had gone out of their way to redo it upon his return to the position of head physician. Within two days of his return to work, the office had been revamped. Whichever decorator they used had captured his style without even bothering to see or question him. He was sure his teammates had a long talk with the woman when James was in recovery, telling her about his likes and dislikes. It was really the only explanation.

Yawning, he took a moment and stretched, his body sore from the position in which he'd fallen asleep. It cracked, creaked and then popped quite loudly.

"Shit. I'm getting old."

Who was he kidding? He *was* old. Maybe not in appearances, but in human years he was ancient, even if he wasn't exactly *that* old as far as supernaturals went.

His night-owl ways had caught up to him. He didn't regret spending his nights chatting online with a woman who made his groin stir to life by doing nothing more than talking to him. She was the only thing keeping him sane. He counted the seconds until they were able to talk, sometimes while playing an online game. He wasn't really a gamer, per se, but he'd learned to hold his own when mentoring young adults. He found he didn't dislike the games either, though he suspected the online company he was keeping had something to do with that.

Still, finding some sound sleep, even for a few hours, would have been welcome. Didn't help that what little sleep he did manage to get was plagued by nightmares. Though, what had woken him with a jolt from his nap hadn't been a nightmare like the others he'd been having since he'd been freed from captivity. Those were basically reliving the torture he'd suffered at the hands of mad men.

This was different.

Much different.

One of his natural-born gifts was having visions. He didn't relish possessing the ability to see the future, and he still couldn't control it, even after all his centuries. His limited control had even wavered more since his time in captivity. It was so far gone now that he was having trouble separating his nightmares from his visions.

Reality from fiction.

The one he'd just had still shook him to his core. The woman in his vision had long black hair with bright purple streaks in it. While it was a strange combination, it worked for her. Her creamy white skin was so pale he'd have thought her a vampire had he not seen her in the sunlight in his vision. The image of her, the sun at her back, her smile wide, her gaze on him, was now burned into his brain. She was quite possibly the single most beautiful woman he'd ever laid eyes upon. Her features were captivating. Her deep, chocolate brown eyes were so dark they bordered on black, and her thick lashes had his attention returning to her gaze in the vision—again and again.

He'd probably conjure that image of the woman in his mind whenever he stroked himself to get off. Stroking himself while thinking of her wouldn't be a hardship by any means.

"Pervert."

His cock stirred to life and he had to adjust himself through his tan designer slacks. It felt good to be back in the clothing he preferred. He'd spent nearly a decade in faded, worn jeans and ratty shirts in an effort to blend in with the street element he'd been trying to assist. Since his return he'd not been able to fly out to Seattle and check in on the street kids he'd taken under his wing. Over the years he'd gotten many back on the straight and narrow, some getting degrees, and many were productive citizens.

Some never assimilated.

He couldn't blame them. All of the kids he'd mentored were supernatural in some regard, though most were ignorant of the fact. James had enough Fae in his DNA makeup that he could sense a fellow magik. The shifter side of him allowed him to sniff out weres with ease. It saddened him to leave that world behind, but he'd not totally abandoned it. Years ago, he'd set up safety nets, a system that, should something happen to him, would ensure the supernatural youths on the streets would still be looked out for. That was a good thing since James had been taken captive and tortured for nearly a year.

One of the street kids he'd personally taken under his wing, Inara, had recently mated to a former PSI-Op (Paranormal Security and Intelligence Operative) who now worked for the Immortal Ops Branch. Eadan Daly was a good guy. James had known for years that Inara was destined for Eadan. James's gift of foresight had told him as much. Inara had also taken to drawing pictures of Eadan before she'd ever met him, so there was no room for misinterpretation. They were supposed to be together.

He couldn't help but feel a tiny bit jealous, even when he was elated for them. He'd always longed for a connection like they shared—a mate of his own. There was no use hoping. With as old as he was, the odds were stacked against him that he'd ever cross paths with the woman made for him. He accepted that, even if he didn't like it.

Inara was now safe and mated to a good man. That was what truly mattered. James had seen her in a fatherly light and was pleased she was now off the streets and with a man who could protect her.

"You failed her," he said out loud. James's temper surfaced again, threatening to overtake him, and he kicked one of the stools near him, sending it skidding across the floor of the lab. He hated himself for being such a fool. For being caught off guard and for being captured in an attempt to keep Inara safe. While he'd been successful at that moment in time, keeping her from falling into the enemy's hands, he'd gotten himself captured instead, and Inara had later been taken by the same men who'd held him prisoner. Thankfully, she'd ended up safe and sound.

You should have held on to your rage back then, he thought, remembering the time before he left PSI. A time when he would have never been taken captive with such ease. A time when his temper ruled supreme. He would have fared better when he was ambushed had he allowed himself to simply lose control, but he hated that side of himself.

After the passing of a close friend and fellow teammate, James had changed his ways. He'd carried the label of murderer for a long time. He'd not killed Christopher with his own hands, but he'd allowed his temper to win—and the end result was Christopher's death. A number of higher ups within PSI had demanded James be tried for murder. The Director, General Jack C. Newman, had come to his rescue, refusing to permit James to be made a scapegoat for the system's failures.

Newman had asked James to stay on and return to duty, but James had refused, needing time to clear his head. Time to pay for the wrongs he'd done. To pay for Christopher's death.

Don't return to being that man. No matter how tempting it might be.

He'd spent ten years on his own, soul searching, making peace with things he could not change and embracing the here and now. He'd lived a good, simple life. He'd learned to control his darker side—his temper.

His thoughts drifted back to the woman from his most recent nightmarish vision. He certainly did not see this woman in a fatherly light at all. His cock still ached with need just from reflecting on her image. The cruel irony being there was a distinct possibility he'd dreamed her up.

He wasn't sure of anything anymore. His

fucking mind was even turning on him. As if he hadn't been through enough as it was. Now he had to deal with possible hallucinations?

What next?

Asking would only mean he'd get an answer and the Fates liked to mess with people. He clearly had a target on his back as far as they went. They were having a ton of fun at his expense as of late.

The girl from his bizarre dream had felt real enough. She didn't seem invented. If she was real, she was in danger. His visions weren't to be taken lightly. Destiny was an odd bird. He learned never to take it for granted. It tended to carve out a person's path far in advance. Whenever James was given a vision of what a person had in store for them, it was never as simple as it being spelled out. No. His visions were impressions, fast flashes, a strange sense of knowing and sometimes cryptic symbols.

Those were the worst.

The more he thought upon it all, the more he was sure it wasn't some invented dream. It was real and she was in serious trouble. He didn't know who, or what, but something or someone wanted the girl dead. Panic welled in him and his hard-on dissipated. The overwhelming urge to find this woman and protect her at all costs swept over him, taking his breath from him. He had to strain to draw in air as he sat there, knowing there was no real way to find her. He didn't have a clue if she was real, let alone who or where she was.

His hands shook and he had to take a break, closing his eyes, forcing himself to calm down. There wasn't anything he could do for this stranger until he had more information. If there was anything he knew for certain about his supposed gift, it was that it revealed the truth of the matter in its own time. It couldn't be rushed. He'd have to wait until it showed him more. That or he'd need to stumble upon the woman. Unlikely to happen since he rarely left the labs or his office. Finding her would not be easy.

"Talk about a needle in a haystack," he murmured. The sudden, undeniable urge to speak with his newly acquired chatroom friend came over him. "I need to talk to GothGirl."

He stared at his computer screen, desperately wanting the woman he'd come to know only as GothGirl to log in so he could speak to her and hear her sweet voice again. It had been nearly twelve hours since they'd last spoken. Seemed like forever. He was supposed to be gathering information on her for PSI. He'd not been very successful. At least not on finding out anything of importance. He did know all her online gaming preferences, her favorite color, that she loved it when it rained and that she could hack just about anything. He also knew she had a big heart. He'd discovered she liked to look after homeless veterans in her area. She'd only specifically mentioned one of them, but he knew from the way she spoke that she cared for many.

He could relate to that burning drive to help the less fortunate. To see to their needs and expect nothing in return. That was the way it should be. Those who gave their time and money only for photo-shoot opportunities or write-ups in papers were shameless.

GothGirl wasn't like that. He'd had to coax the information from her, and she was understated when telling him bits and pieces of what she did for the homeless near her.

He knew she was a good person. Regardless what PSI officials suspected. He knew better.

A smile touched his lips. He knew other little things about her. Details he considered special but his captain would find useless. It had been only a week since he'd been ordered to look more into a hacker an enemy of PSI had a strange interest in. PSI had techs who did that sort of investigation all the time, but even though they operated daily and dedicated their lives to mastering the virtual realm, they'd failed—epically—to make contact with the target.

GothGirl was smart.

Too smart for the computer geeks and the technology analysts on PSI's payroll to catch. They were probably still scratching their heads, and dusting off their keyboards, wondering how the hell some girl had managed to leave them chasing their tails. And boy, had she. James had heard all about the digital runaround she'd given the men.

He laughed at the thought of it all.

When James's captain, Corbin Jones, had held a briefing, telling the men that their raid on the facility James had been held prisoner at had yielded intel on several persons of interest, one being a hacker, James had perked up, curious to hear what was going on. But Corbin had glossed over the information on the young woman, moving quickly to the next order of business. The captain hadn't had much in the way of details, and seemed more interested in other people they'd found information on within the Corporation's files than the hacker. James's body had different ideas, though, building and driving a powerful need for him to learn more of the hacker.

Unable to let the moment pass him, James had forced Corbin to return to the previous topic—the hacker who had caught the eye of PSI. His teammates had groaned as if he were *that guy*—the one who made the teacher return to a boring topic they didn't want to hear any more about.

In a way, that was exactly what he'd done.

Something deep inside him wouldn't let this pass by. When he'd learned that PSI's very own tech squad had failed to gather much beyond the hacker's screen name and that the person was indeed a *she*, he'd found himself volunteering to do more to track her online. Saying he was intrigued was putting it mildly. James had become obsessed and still was.

Corbin had been skeptical. Rightfully so. Yes, James had more skills with a computer than most of his teammates—especially Duke Marlow, who was a luddite in serious denial—but James wasn't a programmer or anything of the like. With a few questioning glances, the captain had given the assignment to James. And James had spent the last week trying to balance his actual job duties with the mission he'd volunteered for. As head physician at the division branch, he never lacked for something to do. Yes, the facility had other doctors on staff as well, and all were very good and exceptionally qualified, but they all answered to James.

A pang of guilt washed over him as he thought of the person-of-interest. Though, within a few hours of launching his own investigation into her, James had stopped seeing her as that—a POI. She was funny, smart, and he found her incredibly sexy—despite the fact they'd never met in person and he didn't know what she looked like.

"You are hung up on a girl who you don't really know and who doesn't really know you." He grunted, slightly embarrassed by his behavior as of late. "Wait until she finds out you're a werewolf and you work for a secret government agency. Oh yeah, she's going to love you."

In his week on the case he had managed to do what the tech geeks couldn't. He'd not only made contact with her, but he'd been engaging in long, drawn-out, deep discussions with her in private chat rooms. He had a hard time believing she was anything PSI needed to be concerned with, but he'd seen the files. He knew she'd managed to gain the attention of the Corporation, leaving them looking into her, trying to mine for information on her. And if that evil empire had their sights set on her that meant PSI needed to know more about her. Corbin wanted to know if she was friend of foe. If she was working with the Corporation or against them.

It had taken him less than an hour of talking with her to know deep in his bones that she wasn't the enemy. Though, labeling her a friend to PSI would have been a stretch.

Of course, telling the captain he didn't feel like she was a bad guy wouldn't really fly. He needed more to go on.

Proof.

And that was exactly what he planned to gather. Proof. Though, it wasn't going to be a walk in the park. Far from it. GothGirl wasn't the type who warmed up to just anyone. He couldn't blame her.

She seemed to believe the government was out to screw everyone. She probably wasn't entirely wrong. James had been alive enough to see countless administrations come and go. They all had one thing in common—the quest for power. There was a lot to be said for the saying "If a politician's lips are moving, they're lying."

Most didn't have a fucking clue what was really go on in the world. They were power-hungry figureheads who thought they understood what real power was, but had none over what really mattered. A few knew of the existence of supernaturals. Most of those humans who did know thought they were in charge of the situation. That they could manage the supernaturals and keep them leashed. That was laughable. Other politicians were actually supernaturals hiding in the open—maintaining a life in the public eye, hiding what they truly were and fully understanding what the hell was happening in the world around them.

Chaos.

So it was difficult to fault GothGirl for being anti the Establishment. The jury was still out if he was as well. For the last decade he'd sure stood against what it all represented. Now he was back and part of it, hopefully part of the solution, not the problem, but only time would tell for sure.

He wished he had something in the way of control over his Fae side so that he could reach out mystically and *will* GothGirl online. Being born with small bits of Fae in his pack line, James could normally sense magik on others faster than most shifters. He'd also had limited abilities in the persuasion side of things. He couldn't wipe humans' memories or anything that full Faes were often capable of, but James had been able to push out suggestions that humans felt compelled to take. The gift had come in handy over the years. Even that particular gift seemed off late. Everything with him did. He'd lost trust in himself and that was a scary thing for a special operative.

Come online, he silently pleaded.

His screen blinked and then chimed, announcing the arrival of GothGirl in the chat room. James didn't believe for a second he'd really had anything to do with her coming online at that very moment. It was merely a coincidence. Nothing more.

He waited for what felt like forever with as anxious as he was to talk with her, before she finally sent an audio chat request. It wasn't as if he couldn't have issued the request but he didn't want to appear needy to her. He answered the request and grabbed his wireless earpiece and microphone, excited to be able to speak with her again. His entire body seemed to respond to the idea of getting to hear her once more.

"Hello, gorgeous," she said, her voice sultry yet young sounding. She had moxie—he admired that about her. She was an interesting mix of fire and ice, carefree yet reserved in other aspects. He enjoyed the mystery she presented.

From the way she talked, she'd been on her

own for a long time. If he had to hazard a guess, she'd been a street kid, and he knew from experience the streets were not kind to anyone, let alone the young. The kids learned at early ages to avoid putting trust in anyone. The longer they spent on the streets, the harder they were to crack. GothGirl had probably been on them for longer than most.

She'd assured him she was twenty-two, and he had to admit he felt a bit like a dirty old man finding her attractive since he was over four hundred years old. James wasn't like some supernaturals. He didn't dwell in the past, yearning for a time long ago. He liked progress and embraced new technologies. He didn't cling to old ways, or every custom from his motherland. Not that he really had a motherland to speak of. The pack he'd been born into was nomadic and hadn't tended to put down roots for long. Probably why James never grew too attached to anything in his long life.

They hadn't been big fans of showing affection or giving a shit about their younger members. You either survived or you didn't. The weak were weeded out and the strong remained.

Immortality left him looking like he was mid-to late twenties, but some days he felt as old as time. Felt like he'd seen and done too much to find joy in anything. GothGirl changed that. She made him feel young again.

Made him feel alive.

Made him laugh.

Made him look forward to whatever interactions, even if only short-term, that they could have.

"You do realize that I may, in fact, be less than pleasant to look at," he said, taking a seat on the stool in his lab. His leg wasn't fully healed from his time as a prisoner of the Corporation, and he had a hard time standing for long periods.

"Oh, you're a hottie. I can feel it," she said.

"Sure," he returned, not really thinking of himself as a catch.

Women found him attractive, but he never understood why. He lacked the arrogance his teammate Duke had. Striker, another of his teammates, also believed himself to be the gods' gift to women. Corbin was more understated in his sexual appeal—like James. Malik, a teammate who was still on forced leave to clear his head, was very secure in his ability to charm the pants off the ladies. Boomer was a different story. There was a certain vulnerability to him that women found irresistible, and Boomer did nothing to discourage the attention.

"I can hear you doubting yourself," she

said, her voice light. “I’m telling you, I know I’m right. You’re a hottie.”

“What about you? Do I get to guess what you look like?” he asked, his mind suddenly trying very hard to make her look like the woman from his vision. He pictured her hair long and dark with purple streaks running through it. Her eyes nearly dark as midnight and as captivating as well. Like normal, whenever he spoke to her his body responded, humming with desire, with the idea of having more than just conversations with her.

“Sure, but I bet you get it wrong,” she said with a sharp outtake of air. “Plus, I’m not really bombshell material. Just a heads up.”

He doubted that very much. In his mind, she was the sexiest woman alive and he wanted to shout at her to recognize that.

Slow down there, buddy, your wires are all crossed because of what was done to you. Don’t let that mess with your better judgment.

"But I can sense that you're a looker," she said with energy that was infectious.

It took him a second or two to gather his control again. Something he seemed to lose a lot whenever anything to do with GothGirl came up.

"One way to know if you're right or not," he persuaded. Part of his mission involved gathering as much intel on her as possible, and that included a picture. He felt like an ass continuing to pursue the mission in regards to her. James liked the woman. *More* than liked her. He wanted to get to know her more than he wanted information on her to pass to others. He wanted to put a face with the voice. "And I'd like to see you."

"Patience, grasshopper," she said. "I'm still considering it from the last time you asked. You know, about thirteen hours ago."

Something baser in him was on the verge of pushing too far to get a glimpse of her, and he worried if he dared let that side of himself out, he'd scare her away for good. She'd go to ground, and if PSI was lucky, they'd find her before the Corporation.

If not…

He didn't want think on that. He couldn't. He'd spent months held captive by them and knew what sick sons-of-bitches they were. Donavan Dynamics—or the Corporation, as they were more commonly known—was about as bad as they came, but by all outward appearances they were pillars of the community, leaders in the search to help rid mankind of disease.

Bullshit.

They were nothing more than mad scientists bent on creating a super race and ending humans for good. Funny the lies humans believed when money was involved. They thought the Corporation was there to help them. In truth, if the Corporation had their way, humans would be nothing more than food for supernaturals.

Cattle.

“Did I lose you?” GothGirl asked.

“No. Still here, tripping over my own thoughts.” He ran his hands over the keyboard before him, wondering again what she looked like. He had real mysteries to solve, yet he found himself obsessing over what some hacker looked like.

“How are the nightmares?” she asked, trepidation in her voice.

James stiffened. He’d not told his teammates that he was suffering from nightmares. They worried enough about him as it was. He didn’t want to add to it all. Seemed as if they took turns checking in on him. He wasn't really sure why he'd confided the truth of it all to her. "I managed to get some rest after we finished talking this morning. Then I had to haul my tired ass into work."

"Work blows," she said with a snort. "Or so they tell me. I'm not really one who has what another would call an honest profession."

"You're really a cat burglar, aren't you?" he questioned, already knowing she was a hacker.

"Guilty."

He smiled and realized he did that a lot whenever he spoke to her. She had become something of a lifeline to happiness for him.

You're lying to her to gather intel on her, he reminded himself. *When she finds out, she'll drop you in a heartbeat and probably never surface on the grid again.*

"Making any headway in your research?" he asked. She'd told him bits and pieces of what she was working on. He'd filled in the blanks on his own. She was painting a huge target on her back as far as the Corporation was concerned.

"Oh yeah. A lot. I accessed another server from the Evil Giant whom I shall not name," she said, making worry lance through him. "I'm running my decryption program on it now. I should have something juicy within twenty-four hours. How is work going for you? Any luck with the samples you were looking more into?"

He'd confessed to being a doctor, but he could sense that she hadn't believed him when he'd told her as much. "Not really. Sort of stuck in a rut with them. I'm thinking I can't see the forest for the trees right now."

"Step back and take a breather then, LabLupus," she said, using his screen name. "I should call you Doc Wolf. Means the same thing, huh?"

He grinned.

If you only knew.

"I feel like I should howl or something," he said, wishing he actually still could. He missed his wolf.

He'd not been able to shift since he'd been captured. The samples that were currently stumping him were his own. He couldn't figure out what the Corporation had done to him. Whatever it was, it changed his genetic make-up, altering him to the point he didn't have a clue what to expect.

"Are you wearing a lab coat?" she asked, a teasing, sexy note in her voice. Her question pulled him from his thoughts.

"Ah, we're going to take the conversation there, are we?" he asked, hopeful. He'd gladly permit the conversation to enter bedroom territory. Hell, it would make his week.

She laughed softly, the sound filling him to

the brim with happiness, something he'd sorely lacked for nearly a year. "Hey, I'll admit to finding it sexy when a guy wears a lab coat. I'm a total kink that way."

"Oh yeah. Nothing says hard-core kinkster than a doctor fetish," he mused, making her laugh more.

"Found me out," she said, and then huffed. "Honestly, I'm not what anyone would label kinky." She was quiet for a bit. "I don't have a lot of experience when it comes to men."

James paused. Was she saying what he thought she was saying? "You have been with a man before, right?" He wasn't sure he wanted to hear the answer. The idea of her being touched by another did what nothing else seemed to be able to do, tempt his inner beast. As a natural-born werewolf, he should have been a force to be reckoned with. Of late, he was about as useful as a human.

He shuddered at the thought. Humans were pretty worthless when it came to anything of importance.

"Um, does our chat room teasing banter count?" she asked.

James palmed the counter before him, pleased with her response. She had not been touched by other men. "No."

"Then no."

He smiled wide. The news of her saving herself moved him in a strange way—he shouldn't have cared about her sexual life choices. They were her choices after all, and he'd seen too many men think they knew what was best for a woman and her body to dare do the same. Yet, he found great pleasure in hearing she'd not let just any ole man touch her. "Good."

"I gotta jet," she said with a tiny moan that turned him on even more. "I just wanted to talk to you quick. Will you be on later?"

"I will," he said, wanting her to remain on the line. Her voice soothed him and helped chase away his overthinking.

"Take care of you, Doc Wolf."

"You too, GothGirl."

She ended the chat and James suddenly felt very empty without her voice in his ear. He craved every moment he could get with her, even though they were virtual moments. Her voice always seemed to wrap around him, making his body tingle with need and his cock ache for release. He'd not wanted another like this ever. Hell, he hadn't even come close to this level of desire before, and he'd been around a long time.

Get a fucking grip, Jimmy, he said to himself.

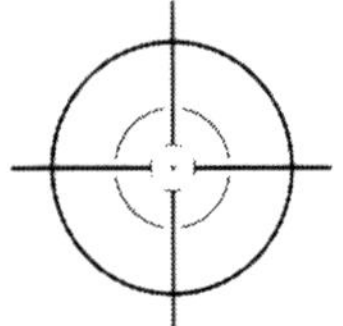

Chapter Two

Doctor Bertrand paced before the window of the rather unimpressive apartment he'd been calling home for the past week. How could anyone live this way? At least the smell of the rotting corpse was gone. Had the previous resident of the apartment simply listened and obeyed when Bertrand and his men had ordered him to be silent, he might still be alive.

Bertrand laughed. Who was he kidding? He'd have killed the man regardless. His lip curled as he looked around the apartment, noting the distinct lack of high-end furnishing he was accustomed to. He'd been living the good life, but all that changed. When he'd tried to reach out to the Corporation for help after the raid in France, his calls had gone unanswered. It was days before he had been able to get a response, and it wasn't the one he was expecting. They blamed him for it all. Claimed he had lost sight of the vision and the mission.

That animal had reduced him to this. Had left Bertrand living just shy of the gutters.

"He shall know no mercy," he said with brutal detachment.

Test Subject 87P.

Though, the test subject had a name now

to go with the face. He was no longer a number.

Dr. James Hagen.

Bertrand went to the broken mirror, hanging tilted from the wall. Peeling wallpaper that had yellowed with age lay partially over one corner of the mirror's edge. How any could live this way—permitting their surroundings to be as such—was a mystery to him.

Bertrand's lips curved upwards, revealing his now-jagged teeth. They had changed when his anger had overtaken him just over two weeks ago. Prior to that, the injections he'd been giving himself—a mixture of varying strands of supernatural DNA and other ingredients known only to him—had been working, increasing his strength, his stamina, his vision, his hearing. But that had all changed when he found himself enraged. He had become what looked back at him in the mirror now. Some sort of disfigured monster. Worse even than the hybrids he and the others like him had been working so hard on creating.

An abomination.

But a powerful one.

He stared at his reflection, no longer recognizing himself as the man he had been. His skin was gray, his face drawn. A ring of red surrounded his irises. Sores had started to form on his skin, pus-filled and swollen. His hair had been falling out in clumps, leaving it patchy at best. He was something to be feared now, as it should be. He was no longer weak. No longer something less than those he studied and experimented on.

He was a force unto himself.

One they would all learn to respect, as they had not done before. Even his higher-ups had laughed at him, mocking his drive to find ways to turn ordinary humans—those lacking any traces of supernatural in their bloodlines—into something more.

But Bertrand had done it. He was living proof.

Running his tongue out and over his teeth, his eyes lit with excitement as he thought of the look upon his immediate supervisor's face when Bertrand had revealed himself and his accomplishments. He'd done so after finally being responded to following the PSI raid on his labs. Right after his favorite test subject managed to get away.

It all came back to Hagen. After all, it had been Hagen's DNA that had made Bertrand's tests upon himself a success after so many failures.

Sharp talon-like claws extended from the ends of his fingers, bringing with them biting pain and torn flesh. Bertrand hissed, spittle dripping from his mouth as he stared down at the ripped ends of his fingers and the twisted claws now there.

He had seen hundreds of shifters do something similar and their changes had been effortless—without blood, without twisted claws.

He would find Hagen, and he would force the man to fix him. Force him to figure what had gone wrong and make it right. Make him a superior being.

Mother Nature was a bitch who wasn't fit to decide who among those brought into this world should and should not be granted special abilities. Bertrand had beat her—he'd beat the grand system of order.

He was now powerful too.

And soon enough, he would have his answers and his cure to make him just as the others he'd spent so long studying. Hagen would do as Bertrand bid. He'd been so close to breaking Hagen's spirit before, that he knew he could do it. And now he had the perfect way to get the man to fold.

A woman.

Bertrand had found a weakness in the good doctor and he would exploit it. He would make Hagen watch as the Corporation's strike teams tore apart the woman Hagen had been so drawn to since his escape.

The hacker.

Bertrand spat and then looked at himself again in the mirror, pleased with the plan he had underway. Gisbert would have to listen to reason once Bertrand showed him that he'd fixed what had gone wrong.

He stiffened, remembering his mentor's harsh words.

"You are a hideous monstrosity," the man had said. "What have you done to yourself?

You were not compatible, not pre-selected. You were merely human."

Merely human.

The words still stung.

Bertrand would fix the problems with his change. He would show the man he had spent years trying to impress with his brilliance that he was a genius. That he too was a leader in the field of genetic manipulation. That he was more than merely human.

He and the men still loyal to him would show them all. They would be welcomed back into the Corporation's fold with open arms and hailed as heroes for not only unlocking the secrets of making humans into supernaturals, but for bringing down the very same PSI team that had laid siege to one of their facilities.

Oh yes.

Bertrand would earn their respect and they would have no choice but to take him back—to stop shunning him as an embarrassment to their master plan.

Rage settled over him as he thought about the Corporation's mission. They wanted a master race of supernaturals to rule the world. They had spent centuries trying to build their dream and see their vision to fruition. They had experimented on natural-born supernaturals, men and women with small traces of supernatural in their bloodlines, and even fetuses still within their mothers' wombs, gaining great success on all fronts, but they had never, as of yet, been able to make an already established human—with no traces of supernatural DNA in their line—into anything more than they started as.

Until now.

Until Bertrand.

He had done the unthinkable. He had managed to make himself more than human.

Yes, there were certain issues that needed addressed, but he would fix them soon enough. As soon as he broke Hagen's will to live. Then the man would aid him. He would do as he was told. He would make Bertrand right.

A supernatural so powerful that all others bowed to him.

A knock sounded on his door and he turned, watching as one of his loyal guards entered. The man cast his gaze downward and Bertrand knew it was because of how he looked—how disfigured he was since he'd begun the change.

"What is it?" he demanded acidly as his gaze narrowed with contempt.

The man shuffled his feet back and forth. "The computer guy says he has a lock on another conversation happening between the target and the girl."

Bertrand laughed.

The girl was the very same hacker who had drawn the attention of the Corporation months ago when she began prying into them. How ironic that she was the woman Hagen had become so obsessed with. When Bertrand ended her he would be doing the Corporation a favor.

He'd be ridding them of the tiny buzzing fly they had been swatting at.

The hacker.

And in doing so, Bertrand would bring down Hagen. It was the perfect plan. One PSI would never see coming. They were arrogant, thinking themselves above reproach. Thinking they were safe on their home soil.

They had no idea the strides the Corporation had been making in recent years. Of how figureheads who normally could not be in a room together had set aside their differences and started focusing on the same goals—ridding themselves of Paranormal Security and Intelligence and the Immortal Ops all while building a master race of super soldiers that when ready, would take over the world and put humans in their place.

The bottom of the food chain.

He looked to the guard. "Report what you find. Be ready to strike. And remind the others, they are to kill the woman and bring me her body. I want to make sure to gift wrap it for a *friend* of mine."

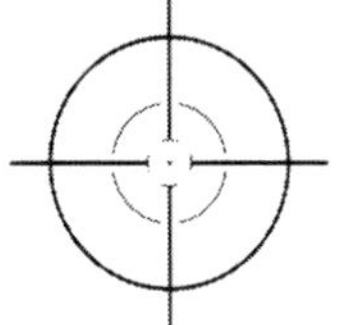

Chapter Three

James touched the top of his microscope, but didn't look at the sample again. He'd been staring at it for days and still couldn't wrap his mind around what he was seeing. He'd been a healer of some sort or another for the majority of his immortal life. He'd seen a lot come and go and had been around for endless technological advances. Hell, he'd even been consulted during the creation of the Immortal Ops, his expertise used to help sort out problems in the program. But what he had before him managed to confound him.

Worse yet.

The sample was from himself. It was one of many he'd taken and that had been taken from him since his return to PSI.

"Sick fucks," he mumbled.

Whatever the hell the Corporation had done to him during his time in captivity there defied all logic. And certainly made little sense to him. Which was scary because he'd completed medical school four times in his lifetime and had also gone to school for science. He'd reinvented himself numerous times throughout his long life—as immortals had to do in order to avoid raising suspicions of humans—and each time he almost always fell back into the role of healer.

Though, once, to his fellow PSI-Ops' dismay, he did attempt to be a hot-dog-stand owner. He'd wanted a change of pace, a less stressful job and to simply stop and enjoy life. Turns out, he wasn't very good at it. Striker had even asked if he was actually cooking honest-to-the-gods dogs as the end quality was greatly lacking.

So, James had returned to what he was an expert at. Medicine.

And if someone with his skillset couldn't make heads or tails of the samples before him, there was a serious problem. From the information he'd gathered, they'd enhanced his natural-born abilities, yet James suffered the opposite effects. His healing ability was stilted. He couldn't shift forms any longer and his senses seemed dulled.

Something was very wrong.

He just wasn't sure how or why.

In need of assistance, James had reached out to the Immortal Ops lead doctor, Thaddeus Green, sending him samples as well. In return, Green had requested his assistance on samples taken from a crime scene in Seattle. The two had been working to try to make sense of the data before them. The I-Ops had a mess on their hands.

Not that PSI didn't.

The Corporation was public enemy number one now at all PSI branches around the world. His team had shifted their focus to find other locations owned and operated by Donavon Dynamics and find out what they were doing there. If it was the same torture and testing as the facility in France, PSI would shut them down.

That is, if they could find them all.

From everything coming to light, the Corporation was huge and far-reaching, hiding under many different names and governments. They more than likely had a hand in the shit in Seattle with a group of bad guys banding together to bring in something that could wipe out hundreds of people—a supernatural the likes of which they'd never seen before. Something capable of leaving nothing but carnage in its wake. The I-Ops and PSI-Ops were overwhelmed but working hard to try to get ahead of the situation.

"Easier said than done," he said softly. Talking to himself in the lab was old habit.

Despite the amount of samples and information coming back, there were still more questions than answers as to what had gone down on the pier in Seattle. James had read the reports and even gotten first-hand accounts from his fellow teammate, Duke. Not to mention Eadan Daly, a PSI Operative who was now an I-Ops team member, had also given his side of it all.

None of it added up.

Whatever the I-Ops were dealing with was powerful and a hodgepodge of supernatural mixes. It wasn't just one, or a hybrid of two different types of supernaturals. The tests were inconclusive, but what they did show said there was a whole heap of shit thrown into whatever had slaughtered all the bad guys who had remained.

Sure, that was no great loss to mankind. Walter Helmuth was a slimeball who ran the Seattle paranormal underground, and he could stand to lose a hell of a lot more of his thugs, but the sheer carnage left at the scene spoke to the trouble this could bring should it happen upon humans.

That was something both the I-Ops and PSI were trying to prevent.

James hadn't been on the docks in Seattle

to help, or even working at PSI again when the attack occurred. No. He'd been locked up in a cell, in the Corporation's French location, undergoing test after test and endless torture at the hands of madmen. His body was still trying to heal the after-effects of it all.

James focused on the samples before him. He didn't want to think about his time in captivity. Duke and Eadan had certainly killed their fair share of bad guys, but they'd then left the dock area and headed to safety. The number of dead found the next morning by the cleanup teams didn't line up with what had gone down. The I-Ops had requested that only select PSI operatives be given the data they'd retrieved. James could understand why. PSI had at least one traitor in its midst.

Possibly more.

The I-Ops had one as well. Somewhere, in the chain of command, someone was double dealing.

One of the monitors nearest James flickered on from sleep mode and was accompanied by a chiming noise, indicating he had a video call coming through. He stepped to the side of his current work area and touched the screen, accepting the call, though he didn't feel much like conversing. He'd been successfully hiding in his labs since his return to PSI.

Green's face came into view. James and Green hadn't known one another long but he'd heard good things about the guy and trusted him because Eadan trusted him. That was good enough for James. Green's auburn hair was clipped nicely as if he wasn't the type of guy who liked anything out of place. James could relate. He too leaned more on the side of clean-cut. That had been one thing he'd missed most during his days on the streets, trying to assimilate and look as though he belonged.

"PSI Freaks and Geeks Central Office. We aim to please and if we don't please, we still keep aiming—usually with a sniper rifle," said James with a wink. "Sometimes, we're even known to hit our target. Depends on how much partying we did the night before, though. What can we do you for?"

Green smiled. "We have a similar motto. Though ours is normally prefaced with, beware or Roi will pee on you to mark his territory since he's not really housebroken yet."

James had run-ins with Roi Majors years ago and didn't doubt for a second he was still a handful. There was a point in time the man was a loose cannon. That had simmered some with his mating.

James put his weight on his better leg. "What's up?"

"We've been working on this end all

through the night with these samples you sent," said Green. "By all outward appearances the male in question should have strength beyond the normal for a shifter and should heal at a rate that basically equals a blink. The Fae component of his blood, that you told me he was born with, should have increased as well. You said the subject is actually in a weakened state and healing is halted?"

The subject was James himself, though he'd not included that tidbit when he'd sent Green his samples. He wasn't ready for everyone to know just how weak he truly was and how damaging his torture had been. "Yes. Also, the male in question can't shift forms."

"And he's natural-born?" asked Green, a low whistle following. "This doesn't make any sense. He should be able to shift faster and be even larger in shifted form than he was before this all occurred. Could the inability to shift and heal fully be psychosomatic?"

James stiffened. Yes, but admitting his problems were all in his head and not the results of the experiments and torture he'd been on the receiving end of while being held captive wasn't a place he was currently at. He pressed an even look to his face. "Possibly."

"As for the other samples, from the holding cells," Green said. "We're finding some interesting results that go hand in hand what your Dr. Mercy there told everyone in her debriefing. The prisoners she knows by the names Brad and Vic had high levels of shifter coming back from their samples, and I'm finding trace amounts of Fae DNA in there as well, but since they were gone when your team raided the establishment, and none of us have been able to find them, I can't say for certain this is their DNA or cross contamination."

James nodded. Made sense.

Green moved awkwardly. "Another thing. One of my teammates, Wilson Rousseau, came in while I was testing the samples. He glanced over the charts and my notes. When he came across the names Brad and Vic, he told me about his time being held by Gisbert Krauss's men in South America."

James waited, wondering where the story was going.

Green continued. "Wilson said there were two graduate students who had been taken down there and held prisoner in the same holding facility as him. He said they were tested on and then moved right away, before anyone could rescue them."

James paused, considering what Green was saying. "If they're the same two that were being held near me, then they've been in the clutches of these assholes a long time."

"Too long," said Green in a hushed breath.

"You all make any advances on any other facilities the Corporation might be using?"

"The massive amount of data we retrieved is all encrypted," answered James. "Our tech teams are working on it but it's pretty sophisticated. They're getting bits and pieces here and there."

Green nodded. "This is big."

"And inter-related to what you guys have going out over there," said James. "It's a cluster fuck."

"And then some," added Green.

James asked another question. "Was there anything more you found?"

"That is all we've come up with so far. We got hit with some hard news so we're not functioning at full capacity right now," said Green. He touched his brow. James knew what had the man worried. PSI had been told about the I-Ops finding out a teammate that had been presumed dead and even buried was neither. James couldn't imagine what the men were going through. He suspected they'd pull away and become harder to contact as time wore on. They just had too much on their plates.

"Have you made any headway on the samples I sent from Seattle?" asked Green.

"I'm retesting what you sent. I'm picking up trace amounts of just about every type of supernatural known to us," he said, still unable to believe the readouts.

"Yeah," Green said, sighing. "We are too."

"This is bad."

Green nodded. "Really bad."

No more words needed said on it. They all knew shit was about to hit the fan and they could only hope it was contained to Seattle. "Your team all back from out there?"

"Yes. Colonel came back with a wife," said Green with a wide grin.

James had to force himself to smile was well. That was what would be expected of him. He didn't feel the same emotions he once did. He felt dead inside. Like a man going through the motions with no real rhyme or reason. "Found his mate?"

"More like finally manned up and claimed the woman he already knew was his mate. Word around here is that you know her," returned Green. He stepped to the side and a woman James hadn't seen in nearly a year appeared in the view. Her long, red, curly hair was down and pretty much going in all directions. It suited her. Always had. She was quite the wild woman.

As he processed why she of all people would be in I-Ops headquarters, he snorted. "Jinx, you're Colonel Brooks's mate?"

"Yes," she said, returning his expression before hers saddened almost instantly. "Oh,

Jimmy, I'm sorry. I didn't know you were missing all those months. I thought you'd done what you always do—gone silent and underground for long bursts. Had I known, I'd have called for help."

He flinched, not wanting to dwell on his time being held captive by the Corporation or the tortures he'd endured. "I'm good."

Jinx didn't look convinced. Probably because he was far from good. His body hadn't healed the damages done to him, and while it had only been just shy of two weeks since he'd been freed and resumed his position with PSI, he should have been back to normal. He'd gotten transfusions from his fellow PSI operatives, and those should have kick-started his own body's ability to heal. As a natural-born shifter male, he could take a lot of damage and his body could repair itself normally within a day or two. A week at most.

He was far from fine. The cane at his side reminded him of that.

"Can I do anything at all to help?" Jinx asked, concern lacing her every word.

They'd been friends a long time. He was happy she'd found a mate, but slightly envious as well. It was hard not to be at his age. He'd been alive a long time and doubted he had someone special out there, destined for him.

No.

He'd burned up his goodwill with karma years ago.

"I'm fine, really, Jinx. Congratulations on your mating," he said, his hands moving to the countertop to support his weight. He didn't want to have to sit on the stool near him and show his weakness to others. "I'm dying to know what Brooks is going to do about you and that club of yours. Somehow, I'm doubting he's going to let you keep running it."

Jinx blew out an annoyed breath. “That jerk is telling me I can’t go back and run my own place. I think he wants me barefoot and pregnant here with him.”

James laughed softly. “I’m guessing he just wants you safe and close to him.”

“If you say so,” she said, partially under her breath. “He’s an alpha douchebag.”

“Ah, but he’s your alpha douchebag,” James reminded her.

“Dammit,” she said with a smile.

Green guffawed behind her. “Colonel has made other arrangements for Jinx’s club. It will remain open but it’s being guarded by a whole lot of men now.”

Jinx waved a hand in the air and rolled her eyes. “I can handle my own place.”

James knew how headstrong Jinx was. It was part of her charm. But with the readouts he had in front of him and the samples that surrounded him, James knew better than to permit someone he cared about to put themselves in harm's way. "Jinx, listen to Brooks on this. There is some seriously bad juju out there right now. If I was you, I'd ask the club be closed, at least until we get a handle on it all."

Jinx paused and then neared the camera on her end more. "It's really that bad?"

"Yes."

"Aneta is taking over the club for me," she said, her voice tapering off. "Is she safe there? Are my girls safe?"

James considered lying to her, but they'd been friends too long for him to do it. "No. Not even with the extra security. Get them out of the there, Jinx. Take them to your backup location in New Orleans."

Green leaned in and looked at Jinx. "You have another club in New Orleans?"

She blushed. “I do.”

“Does Brooks know this?” asked Green.

Jinx pursed her lips. “Um, not really.”

Green groaned. “Colonel bit off more than he can chew with you, didn’t he?”

That brought a smile to Jinx’s face. “He did, and I’ll go tell him to arrange relocating my girls and my boys to New Orleans right away.”

“Why is it you listen to Hagen, but not your own mate?” Green asked, a devilish look on his face. The man was toying with Jinx.

“I like to make Asher work for it,” supplied Jinx with a shrug of her shoulders. She glanced at James. “Do you need one of my girls to come to you? Sex can sometimes speed the healing process.”

James’s arms began to strain from holding himself up. “No. Thank you, though. I haven’t used the services your girls provide in years.”

"Over a century, Jimmy," she corrected.

Had it been that long?

She didn't give a chance to respond. "Don't give up hope on meeting *her*. I think she's closer than you know."

He didn't need cryptic messages. He had enough to worry about.

"I'm good, Jinx. Take care of yourself and your people. Let us work on solving what is going on in Seattle and in the meantime, try to listen to your husband," he said before touching the screen and ending the video call.

James practically fell onto the stool, the pain in his leg past his threshold.

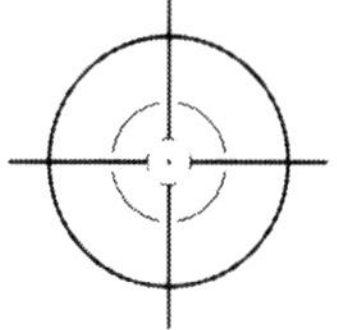

Chapter Four

Laney Steele sat before her modified, souped-up computer system. It was a work of art. The envy of her small network of fellow computer people. Dr. Frankenstein himself would be in awe of what she'd pieced together and brought to life. Of course, her creation had a lower than likely chance of being chased down by peasants with pitchforks, but still, it was pretty awesome. If she did say so herself.

Plus, if her system ever did manage that level of animosity from people, that would only up her cool factor among other computer geniuses.

Put a stamp of approval on all her hard work.

GothGirl kicks major system ass.

She currently had eight monitors, four sitting in a row before her and four others mounted above those. The refresh rates were top notch, as was everything to do with her system. Each monitor displayed something different, though they could flow into one another with the same data should she choose to do so. Cooling fans were installed around the system because of the heat it kicked. Didn't matter much that she had extra internal fans in each CPU. The additional cooling was required. Her system ran that hot.

"Just like me," she mused softly. "Hot

mama."

Laney nearly laughed herself right off her comfy computer chair as joy continued to bubble through her. She was hardly a sex kitten. No. She'd been honest when telling LabLupus that she was far from bombshell material. Her best buddy, Harmony, wore that title with honor and pride. Laney was more the weird chick who looked slightly Goth but was really just too lazy to bother buying anything more than a select few colors. Not that she needed much in the way of clothing. She wasn't a frilly girl. And her attire kept people at a distance. As she preferred. She wasn't exactly the most social of girls.

She spent her money on her computers and technologies. Not on clothes, purses, shoes or makeup. What extra she managed to obtain she was sure to pay forward—to those who couldn't do for themselves anymore.

Her boys.

She smiled slightly, thinking of how they were hardly boys. The men who resided in the building with her. Fellow squatters. Her neighbors.

Laney wasn't sure what she'd do without them all. They were something of a family, as mismatched as they may be. She checked in on them nearly daily, making sure they had what they needed, as most tended to be shut-ins.

Her duties for the day in regards to the two who needed to be looked in on the most—Gus and Bill—were done. She'd made sure both of them had food, had what they needed in their rooms, and that they were settled for the day. Gus liked books and Laney visited the library twice a week to get him different ones. Bill enjoyed building model planes. She'd picked up a new one for him. He'd be at it for days and days.

Now she was free to do what it was she did.

Search for the truth.

She looked around at her computer system, what she'd invested most of the money she kept for herself. It seemed as though a small fortune was in it. Well, it wasn't exactly her fortune she'd invested, but still.

She'd amped up everything and had spent years building the perfect machine. She didn't want to think on the cost. Some she'd bartered for. Some she'd worked for, and others she'd helped herself to a five-finger discount—not really, because she didn't actually go and lift it from the store. She was a master of theft, and overriding ATMs was a go-to way to get cash for her. She only took from those who had plenty to give, and sometimes she even played the part of the Robin Hood, though she doubted the authorities or die-hard do-gooders would see it that way.

"They'd lock my butt up for sure," she said, with a grunt.

She wasn't exactly proud of how far she'd fallen from the perfect suburban, middle-class child she'd once been. That had all been a lie. A big fat front to hide who and what she truly was.

An engineered super freak.

Laney wasn't entirely sure how she came to be, but in her mind it involved test tubes and growing in a glass jar. Though she knew she had a mother, or at least a woman who had carried her to term. She often wondered if the woman had loved her or if Laney was merely a way to make money, or worse, something the woman was forced to carry. Laney would bet her hard drives that Mother Nature had very little to do with it all.

Her hands began to shake and she closed

her eyes a moment, chasing away her inner demons. She looked up at her system again. It was the envy of any serious programmer. Her code-writing abilities far surpassed others out there and she wasn't afraid to let them know. Naturally, they knew her by GothGirl, not her name—or rather the name that had been put on her adoption papers. Laney had a better ring than Female 43867, the name that was originally labeled on the paperwork she'd uncovered. Guess she could at least send her adoptive parents a thank-you card for going above and beyond with the whole giving-her-a-real-name bit.

She looked down at her fingers as they swiped across the keyboard with a speed others simply did not possess. Her adoptive parents had gotten more than they'd bargained for. By age twelve Laney's hacking had gotten her assigned to house arrest. The ankle bracelet that had been placed upon her to monitor her activities was a joke. She'd found a way around it within twenty minutes of it being placed upon her person. More like ten minutes, but she'd then spent the next ten tweaking it to show her as moving within the dwelling, even though the ankle bracelet was stationary on her bedroom shelf.

Of course, it wasn't long after that her parents had thrown their hands in the air, unable to deal with her. She was too much of a handful and was always finding trouble in places trouble shouldn't have existed. At least that was what their parting words had consisted of.

They aren't your real parents, she thought. A coldness settled into her chest as she thought upon the information she'd uncovered about her origins.

She couldn't go to that dark spot again.

She'd only just begun to dig herself out of a pit of emotional despair. Harmony, who also happened to be a fellow computer enthusiast, would slap her upside the back of the head if she dared to allow herself to fall into a funk again. It had been two years since Laney had learned the truth of who and what she was, and only a few months since she'd finally stopped throwing a pity party for herself.

Snap out of it.

Normally, she'd preferred to spend her evening in, mining for data on the servers she'd recently discovered, and then spend some time online upping her status in her favorite role-playing game. She was almost to the highest level and an asset to her gaming league, especially since she was the team healer. Without her, the rest of the guild wouldn't get too far in a battle.

In real life she was hard-pressed to do

much beyond look at an injury, even a slight one, and try to keep her lunch down, but in the virtual world, she was whatever she wanted to be. She was someone others cared about and she had more friends than she could tally. In real life, she had Harmony.

That was it.

The only reason she even had Harmony was because the girl didn't take no for an answer. Harmony had tracked Laney down via the net and refused to leave until Laney went out for coffee with her. That was four years ago. They'd been friends ever since.

And Harmony knew the truth about Laney. Of what she'd uncovered in her quest to locate her birth parents. The truth about something the government referred to as the Asia Project. Now it was a matter of tracking down her incubation lab.

"Bitter much?" she asked herself, her

fingers skimming over the keys quickly.

Her gaze scanned the multitude of screens she had before her. It was her small slice of paradise, despite the fact it was in an abandoned hotel that had seen better days and the room hadn't seen the light of days in years. It had everything she needed. She kept the utilities on by simply hacking the providers' servers, making it look as if she wasn't using any power, and when she was, making it appear as if it had been paid in full. The best part was, no one would ever think to look for her there. And the building, which had been slotted for demolition, was safe because Laney made sure to keep an open virtual door to the city's servers, always monitoring for anything being mentioned about the hotel. She'd then hack accordingly, protecting it any way she had to. Besides, as behind as the city had gotten in its attempts to clean up and revitalize the downtown area, they had more important things to worry about than the old hotel.

It was the closest thing to a home she'd ever had and she was damn proud of it. Despite what it looked like or lacked in amenities—pretty much everything. It served its purpose and gave her a place to do what she did best.

Hack.

Information came at a speed most normal people's brains couldn't process, but Laney was hardly what one would term normal. She never had been. She could absorb and sort out data at a rate that would shock most people.

Some called her a hacker. That wasn't exactly true. She saw herself as more of a hackivist—bringing the truth of the government's secret activities to light. People knew of GothGirl—the name but not the person. They knew nothing of the person. Most just called wrote off her theories as crazy. But she knew she wasn't. That what she was trying to bring to light was true.

She was living proof.

People were so narrow-minded, refusing to believe in what seemed impossible yet was anything but. She was proof of that. Plus there was so much more than what she'd found out about herself.

"Blue Butterfly would be proud," she said, thinking of her internet friend she'd met nearly a year ago. They'd never actually met in person, but that hadn't mattered. Blue Butterfly had helped Laney in her search for information on her birth and birth mother. In return, Laney had assisted Blue Butterfly with an encryption program. When Blue Butterfly began to drop hints as to why and for what, Laney took that as permission to start digging on the woman's behalf. That was how Laney learned the truth about what she'd suspected.

Supernaturals were totally real.

There were men who could shift into animals and they worked for the government. She bit at her lower lip as she thought about her latest run-in with a high-ranking government official. She'd waited outside a black-tie event in the pouring rain for hours for a chance to ask the senator about the secret program, only to end up being hauled into the police station and threatened. If she came within fifty feet of the senator again, she'd find herself in jail.

Or so they claimed.

They'd have to find her first. It wasn't like she lived a life on the grid. No. She'd vanished from the system in her early teens and hadn't surfaced again using her own identity since. Laney Steele no longer existed, at least on paper. GothGirl did, but the trail she'd left behind went everywhere and nowhere. It would lead anyone looking into the alias on a wild goose chase of the virtual variety.

A testament to her skills.

The authorities would be chasing a ghost. She took some pleasure in that as she wasn't known for wanting to help *the Man* in any way.

"*The Man* can suck it."

Laney had a distinct and overwhelming dislike of *the Man*—which to her, encompassed government and the real people who were in control of the government—big business and secret societies. They were all in bed together, deciding the fate of people without giving them any say in the matter. They played god with people's lives and they did what they pleased without the public ever knowing what they were really up to. The world was run by bullies who used their armies and hired guns to enforce their secret agendas.

She and her fellow group of like-minded online community were trying to make a difference. Trying to gather in the information they needed to stop it all. Not to mention information Laney needed to make sense of herself.

The screen to her left blinked as a window popped up, alerting her to a hit on one of the scanning programs she had running. The feed came across the screen, first in nothing more than coding, and then, as her decryption program did its magik, actual information, and she smiled. Lists of test subjects scrolled by her. Though they had names like Test Subject 87P, rather than given names. Still, it was something to go off of. More than she'd had yesterday.

Blue Butterfly had vanished from the net about seven months back. For her to leave no virtual trail that Laney could track was a serious worry. Laney was an expert. If Laney couldn't track someone using technology, something was wrong.

"The stupid friggin' *man* probably nabbed her."

Pausing the information flow, Laney looked to the screen and scrolled back to the files for Test Subject 87P, the urge to investigate this particular subject great enough that she couldn't ignore it. She accessed the file, waiting, watching as her program worked its magik, revealing information in increments. At first, it looked to be sequencing something to do with DNA, but she didn't understand it enough to read what she was seeing. Next, her program decrypted detailed chart entries.

Test Subject 87P fought with guards.

Punished.

Test Subject 87P resistant to scientists.

Punished.

Test Subject 87P was denied food or water for three days as a lesson for previous behavior. When guards entered the cell, he attacked them.

Punished.

Test Subject 87P is protective of the females, employees or not. Suspect it has to do with his alpha nature. Will investigate further.

Laney's gut tightened with the seemingly endless lines of information about just how much this Test Subject 87P had been punished. When some of the reprimands were spelled out clearly, she thought she might be sick.

"Oh my god, they're evil," she whispered. "Absolutely evil."

More and more on the subject in question spewed forth onto her screens. She spotted video files and quickly moved out of the area. She couldn't see what they'd done to this man. She couldn't witness it with her own eyes.

Not now.

She'd be sick.

She just knew it.

She'd need an entire bottle of wine before she could even think to open the video files, and even that might not be enough to numb the horror she knew she'd feel as she watched the cruelties this place was capable of.

A bittersweet taste coated her tongue. She'd been mining data for nearly two years on the subject and finally had a breakthrough. She pushed her long, black hair back from her face as she keyed in a few strokes, delving deeper into the newly accessed information. She'd taken to adding purple streaks to her hair and a section of it pushed forward into her face once more. Harmony would tease her if she saw her and tell her to cut her hair and try to be a little more low-key.

As Laney read the information on the test

subject she'd pulled up, her stomach twisted. The doctors and scientists had shown the male no mercy. The world she'd stumbled into had some sick sons-of-bitches in it. The proof was before her.

She was onto to something big.

Really big.

Of course, no one would believe her. Well, no one outside of her online fellow conspiracy theorists. Some of them were total whack jobs though, so she never truly counted them all. Harmony would have a hard time swallowing all of the truth. She tended to take Laney in stride, as did most.

She looked over her current article. It was coming along nicely. She wouldn't put it live until she had more facts to back up her claims. This was a gem, full of information she'd gathered both digitally and with some major boots on the ground. She'd put thousands of miles on her old beater of a car and wasn't sure how long it would hold up. While she had the skills needed to steal a new one out from under the noses of any car dealership, that wasn't her style. She only took when she had no other choice. For all the rest of her needs she hired out her skills and used the money to fund her obsession.

Seeking the truth.

Her attention went to the picture of a giant office building in France. It had recently been the scene of a number of explosions. Of course, the company, Donavon Dynamics, claimed it was an internal error—caused by an employee accidently mixing a catalyst and a cobalt. She wasn't buying their cover story. It was shaky at best and held little water.

The place was built like Fort Knox and from everything Laney could gather on the Donavon Dynamics website, they were extremely selective in their hiring process—they hired the best of the best. She highly doubted they'd hire a moron who would be careless enough to cause an error of that magnitude.

For the past three weeks Laney had been digging up anything and everything she could find about Donavon Dynamics. She had yet to uncover all their dirty little secrets, but she'd linked them to enough already to know they were not on the level. They weren't about doing good for mankind.

Not at all.

With a strong need to find anything else to occupy her mind, Laney logged into one of the chat servers she sometimes frequented. It was a hotspot for fellow conspiracy theorists who also enjoyed gaming.

Her gaze ran over the screen as she searched for one screen name in particular.

LabLupus. It had only been a few hours since they'd last spoken, but she missed the sound of his voice.

He was newer to the forums, but they'd struck up a friendship of sorts in a very short time. She smiled when she saw his screen name there. Within seconds she was invited to a private room by him. She put on her headset and couldn't stop the flurry of butterflies that tickled her belly as he spoke.

"Hey there, GothGirl," he said, a deep timbre to his voice. "I was hoping you'd come back on before too late."

"Miss talking to me?" she asked, silently hoping he did.

"Yes," he said with such conviction that her breath caught. "Every all right?"

Laney didn't exactly want to confess she was elated he'd missed speaking with her. She didn't want to sound pathetic. She'd missed him too. She wasn't sure why he had such an effect on her, but he did. The bond she'd forged with him by simply talking was strong. Stronger than it should be. She understood as much. "Um, yes. Sorry. I wanted to share my good news. I just had a breakthrough in my data mining," she admitted.

"Going to tell me about it?" he questioned, his voice tight.

"It's something that will expose the corruption in big business and how the governments around the world climb into bed with them, letting them do as they please while labeling it scientific advancements," she answered. "Enough of all that. I want to talk about you. You're not still in the lab, are you?"

"I actually enjoy hearing about what you're working on," he said.

She snorted. "Most people just laugh."

"I'm not laughing."

"You didn't answer my question," she said, wanting off the topic of herself. So far, LabLupus was the one person she'd let semi-close who didn't make fun of her for her theories. She wanted to keep it that way if possible. "You're not at work still, are you?"

"Yes. Been in the lab all day going over the same samples," he said, a tightness entering his voice.

Laney sat up more, disliking knowing something was bothering him. While they'd only been chat buddies for a short time and they'd never exchanged pictures or met in person, he was important to her. Very important. She really couldn't explain why. "I'm sorry. I wish I could help you in some way. I know this is important to you even though you won't tell me what exactly it is you're trying to find in the samples."

He was quiet a moment and she feared he

might actually leave the chat. Something close to panic began to rise within her at the idea he might be upset with her and stop speaking to her. As the realization settled over her that she couldn't go a full day without conversing with him, her pulse raced and beads of sweat began to form on her brow.

Holy crapola, I'm really into this dude.

"Thank you," he said, breaking the long pregnant pause that had bloomed in their conversation. "There are certain anomalies I'm attempting to isolate so that I can better understand a few other things."

It was easy to hear he didn't want to expand further on what he was doing. She could respect that. She cleared her throat and decided a new topic was in order. "I wanted to thank you for the suggested reading material on servicemen suffering from PTSD. It's been very helpful."

"The veteran you're refusing to tell me much about," he said softly. "How is he doing?"

"As good as can be expected," she said. "It helps me to understand a little more about what he might be going through. I can't thank you enough. I'll never really get what it's been like to walk in his shoes, to see and do what he's had to do, but now I'm at least better able to try. As a doctor, do you treat a lot of men and women who served?"

A shaky laugh came from him. "You could say that. Also, I've served myself. I can very much relate."

It was difficult to keep from liking the man even more. Laney had a soft spot for veterans. "Thank you."

"For?" he asked.

"Serving," she said.

Dead air seemed to last forever before he

spoke. "I've told you already that if you want, I can come to you—meet somewhere neutral—and see what I can do to help these men. I'm more than qualified as both someone who has been in their shoes and a medical professional."

"How do you know there are more than one?" she asked.

He laughed softly. "Your voice. The things you say to me. Makes me think you're keeping an eye on a number of men who served in the military but who no longer fit into society's norms."

"They're good men," she said a little defensively. She would do anything to protect them.

Anything.

"I know," he returned. "I can tell by the way you talk about them that you care. A lot. That is a good thing. A really good thing.

Sometimes, it can feel like you're totally and completely alone."

"I do care about them," she said, her voice low. "They're like family to me."

"I guessed as much. And I'm happy to hear you've made a breakthrough in your data mining," he said, sounding anything but pleased with the news she'd shared. "Can you tell me anything more?"

"This group I'm looking into is totally screwed up and they need to be stopped," she said, before thinking better of it. "Never mind. It's nothing."

He sucked in a slow breath. A prickle of unease settled over her and she could have sworn it radiated from him. That was crazy. "Tell me what you're working on," he said, a cautious note in his voice.

"You'll tell me I'm nuts. My best friend tells me that daily," she said, hoping to lighten the mood. “The guy your info on PTSD helped me with, he’d believe me, I’m sure of it, but I don’t tell him what I’m doing. He’ll lecture me on the dangers out there and how the big bad wolf will come and eat me for interfering.”

“He’s probably not far from wrong,” he said. “I won’t judge you.”

Laney bit at her lower lip and then decided to give him a small sample of what she’d been doing. “What if I told you I think supernaturals are real?”

“Like Bigfoot?” he questioned, a teasing note in his voice. “I’ve heard there are already teams dedicated to trying to find him. I’m pretty sure he sits in a tree, looking down at them, thinking, ‘Stupid humans’.”

Laney’s cheeks lifted as she smiled wide. “I’m being serious.”

“So am I,” he said. “Okay, so you’re talking more on the lines of vampires and stuff?”

She shrugged. She was about to admit to him, out loud, what got her labeled a nutjob. "Yes. But all kinds of other supernaturals too. Like men who can turn into animals. Werewolves and other were-creatures. Even skinwalkers. Witches. Faeries. Other mythical creatures."

"Go on," he said, something raw in his voice.

"And what if I told you there was a group of powerful companies, certain governments and people that banded together to form a coalition of sorts—a corporation—that while on the outside they appeared normal and helpful, behind it all they were monsters who hurt people and supernaturals? That they want to create a master race? That they have an end goal to make super-supernaturals?" she asked, waiting for him to laugh.

"I'd say it's dangerous to be digging up

information on this corporation and that it would be unwise to continue to put yourself in harm's way."

"You don't think I'm batcrap crazy?"

He spoke, "I think you're painting a target on yourself."

"You sound like Casey," she said.

"I take it Casey is the veteran you wanted information on PSTD for."

Laney stilled. She hadn't meant to say Casey's name. She knew how private he was. How much he didn't want to be on the grid in any way. "Do you believe me?"

"Does it matter?" he asked.

It did. More than it should. "Yes."

"Then I believe you. And I believe this corporation would have to be powerful and willing to do anything to silence someone they viewed as a threat to their coalition. And GothGirl, I would think a young woman mining data in their servers would be viewed as a threat. Do you agree?"

"I guess, but they'd need to know what I was up to and they don't," she boasted. "I'm that good. I get the data I need right under their noses and they're none the wiser."

"Or they want you to believe they have no idea, but in reality they're monitoring you," he returned, sounding very sure of himself.

She tensed. "Maybe. I'm careful though."

"GothGirl," he said, real concern radiating from his voice. "These people don't sound like people you should cross."

Laney reflected a moment, weighing how smart it was to give away information about herself to someone who was technically a stranger. Something deep within told her it was the right thing to do. Harmony was the only other person beside her "boys", as she referred to them, who knew her name. She was about to add one more person to that short list. "Laney. Please call me Laney. It's my name."

"Laney." He hummed softly, the sound making her belly tingle with desire. "That is a great name. Rolls off the tongue much easier than GothGirl."

She smiled. "I understand if you don't want to share your name."

"James, but most people call me Jimmy or Hagen," he said quickly. "Guess it depends on whichever you prefer. I went through a brief spell in the last ten years or so that I picked Jimmy, but honestly, no matter how far I run or how much I try to change, or what someone calls me, under it all, I'm still just me."

Laney ran a hand over her upper chest and leaned in towards her monitor as if she could see him. In reality, she saw only a blank window on her screen with his user name in it. She could have done a search on his name to find out everything there was to know about him, but somehow, in this case, it felt like a violation of trust. No. She'd leave learning about him up to chance, something she rarely did. "Nice to meet you, Hagen."

"Laney," he said softly. "I'd like to really meet you. In person. I realize that may seem unwise given the short time we've been talking, and the fact that while we converse a great deal, we don't know that much about one another."

She enjoyed the way he talked, often as if he were a man out of place in time, while other moments he spoke like he was totally in the know. "I want to meet you in person too. Can you get away and meet for coffee around eight tonight? I know you've been spending a lot of time in your lab and that you want to crack whatever mystery it is you're working on, so I'll understand if you don't want to take time out for this tonight."

"I wouldn't miss it for the world. Where do you want to meet?" he asked.

She licked her lower lip, very pleased that he wanted to see her too. "It's a good thing we figured out we're local our first night talking, or this meet up would take some serious planning."

"True. But you should know, I'd do whatever it took to get a chance to meet you."

She wasn't sure what to say to that, but did know that it warmed her to hear him say it. "Let's meet at *Mugs* on Ninth," she said. "Got a pen? I'm going to give you my cell."

"Go ahead and tell me. I'm good. I'll remember it."

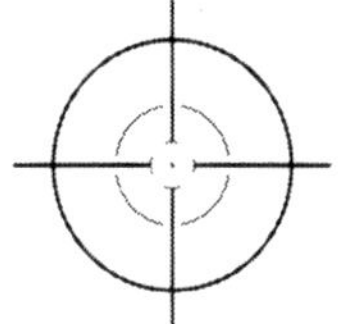

Chapter Five

James found himself humming classic rock tunes as he went back to work, feeling energized after speaking to GothGirl. He had a date with her and he felt like a young man again. He'd not been on a date in so long he only hoped he still remembered how to handle himself.

"Laney," he said in a soft whisper.

He had a name now, and he knew he should notify Corbin of his progress, but he didn't want to share her with anyone. Not even the captain.

She's mine.

He mentally slammed to a stop.

Mine? Where the hell did that come from?

Had the Corporation's experiments on him left him so out of touch with his natural responses that he was now fixating on some random woman—the first woman who caught his interest after his horrible ordeal? Was his body really betraying him in such a cruel way? Giving him false positives on his body's inborn need to lay claim and mate?

The door to the lab swung open so fast it struck the wall. James tempered his elation over his upcoming date with Laney. He raised a brow and looked to the side as two of his teammates entered, arm in arm, swaying as if they might be too drunk to stand.

Knowing them, they were.

Being immortal shifters, the men could pack the liquor away and metabolize it at an extraordinary rate. For them to be in the state they were currently in, they must have drunk a whole hell of a lot. He'd once found Duke, Striker and Boomer asleep on a pile of empty bottles in an alley behind a bar in New York. None of them could remember how they'd gotten there and each smelled like they'd drank their weight in whiskey. It was the early eighties, and whatever had happened that night had left Duke wearing a pair of spandex pants—something he would never wear willingly. That wasn't the best part. Striker had on full makeup and his hair teased all while wearing a t-shirt for a pop-rock band that James knew the guy hated.

That must have been one hell of a drinking

night.

James's mood lit with the memory of it all.

Miles "Boomer" Walsh's long dark hair was down today, and when he entered the room more, the lights caught varying colors running through his hair. In the right light it looked almost blue-black. His unnaturally violet gaze found James and he stopped, causing the man currently hooked to him to nearly fall on his face.

That would have been something to see considering just how big Dougal "Striker" McCracken was. He was easily the biggest of James's team of men. He was currently the hairiest as well. Already there was a challenge going at PSI to see who could convince the guy to shave. So far, no one had won. The auburn-haired giant had given up shaving some time back and resembled a mountain man more than the Scottish Highlands warrior he truly was.

James noted the kilt Striker wore and didn't comment. No point. The man was the type of supernatural who was proud of his heritage, of the long life he'd lived. His friend was more comfortable in kilts and more often than not Striker said fuck it to society and wore one around. Of course, the guy paired it with combat boots because it was Striker and that was his personality. He'd been in jeans most of the week, which made James wonder if tonight was one of Striker's "I miss the motherland" nights.

Songs and odes to William Wallace were sure to follow. James had been on the receiving end of countless conversations where Striker tried to convince him that PSI should get a day off work each year in honor of the fallen hero of Scottish lycans. So far Striker hadn't made any great strides in making that happen.

Wasn't for lack of trying though.

Striker had the kilt paired with a t-shirt that read *Have Stake Will Use It*. The man wore stranger things. James didn't question.

Striker looked up, a shit-assed grin on his face. "Och, lookie, told ya we'd find the doc in here, playin' with nerdy things. Find the beakers, find the doc. A quote we could live by. Well, unless the doc is in hiding for ten years again, then you do nae find jack shit."

James refrained from comment as he had indeed gone to ground for a decade, lying low, going rogue before he'd been captured and held captive all those months. He was back now. That was all that mattered, despite how much it clearly still bothered Striker. Though he did miss some of his street contacts.

Boomer lifted his left arm and clicked his fingers. "You *are* a genius," he said, his speech slurred. He made a move to high-five Striker, but ended up hitting Striker in the side of the head instead.

Striker didn't seem to notice or care. He reached down with his free hand and scratched his ass, thankfully through the kilt, or James was sure he'd have gotten an eyeful of Striker's naked self. Not that he hadn't seen the man naked before. They were shifters after all and had run together when letting their wolves free too many times to count. Still, he wasn't really up for getting a glimpse at the Scot's man parts.

"You're coming out with us tonight," said Boomer, pointing to James. "We're going clubbing."

James hid his groan. Clubbing? They couldn't be serious. "Aren't you already drunk? Wouldn't clubbing be excessive?"

"Och, we're nae drunk. We've never been more sober," said Striker, leaning hard to the right, taking Boomer with him. "We let Mercy try a new sedative on us. Dinnae work though."

Dr. Mercy Deluca, Duke's mate, was gifted in Biomedical Engineering. She'd started working in the Research and Development area of PSI the same day James returned to the fold. She also held a special place in his heart as they'd come through the other side of an ugly ordeal together. So far, in her limited amount of time with PSI, she'd managed to make quite an impression.

Boomer hiccupped. "Made us feel tipsy, but didn't knock us out or anything. She's in there now, trying to amp it up."

"Did you just use the word tipsy?" asked Striker. "Does nae sound verra manly."

Boomer tugged at Striker's kilt. "Neither is wearing a dress."

"Bite me," returned Striker.

Boomer flashed fang. "Gladly."

"You'd get a taste of me and realize nothin' but a Scot will do for you from here on out," said Striker, a serious note to his voice. "My milkshake is that powerful. Brings 'em all to the yard."

James had no idea what the man was talking about. He was just happy that over the centuries Striker's Scottish brogue had lessoned enough to make him understandable on most days.

"Bet I'd get indigestion instead," returned Boomer. He made a grand gesture of rubbing his abs. "And the shits. I'm a werepanther and cats don't tolerate milk nearly as well as people think we do. So, your *milkshake* would fuck up my digestive system."

James shook his head.

"Do nae make me call yer girlfriend," warned Striker, a wicked gleam in his green eyes. "I'll get her sprung from the zoo and the two of you can get some quality cuddle time in. They tell me she's in heat. Should make for a wild ride."

James had heard all about what the other team members had done to Boomer when he'd passed out drunk. They'd carried him in shifted form to the local zoo and put him in the panther exhibit. He woke up with an eager panther female trying very hard to convince him to mate with her. The men had pictures of the entire ordeal and had them framed in the main hallway of PSI. Boomer had even won the famed and unofficial award of *Asshole of the Week* due to the incident.

James had won it many times in his past as well. Most incidents had sprung from his temper. Some were Striker's fault.

Boomer blushed. "I can't help if I'm wanted by the ladies."

"Even the ones who cannae shift and walk on two feet," said Striker with a snort. "If we hurry, we can get you to your hottie before the zoo closes. If yer a good boy, I'll get you a balloon and ice cream when we're there."

Boomer groaned. "There you go with talk of milk products again."

"Gentlemen," interjected James. He licked his lower lip, a laugh wanting to come. Mercy had been using the men of PSI as willing lab rats since she'd been brought on. Her experiments never harmed anyone, but this one seemed to have some interesting side effects.

They were still better than what had happened to the captain while visiting Mercy's office. James nearly laughed at the thought of it all. He paused. "You're not armed are you?"

Striker grunted. "Och, Duke took our weapons before we let his wee slip of a wife inject us. Says we can have 'em back after she's all done with us."

Smart.

"I'm not sure you should be mixing alcohol and sedatives, even with your metabolisms. Seems unwise," added James. He knew if he dared to allow them to leave in their current state they'd unleash pandemonium in the streets of the city. They were trouble on a normal day. Hopped up on Mercy-Juice could only make it worse.

"Bedding those wenches outside the barracks of the English encampment in the late seventeen hundreds was a bad idea," pushed Striker, swaying more. When he managed to regain his footing, he made motions as if he was pumping into a woman when in reality he was using thin air to prove his point about his prowess. "They were screamers, but totally worth it. Woke the whole damn regiment.

Bloody English chased me around when I was in naught more than what I'd been born in."

James actually cracked a full, real smile at the thought of Striker trying to evade the English army. They'd been friends a very long time and been through quite a bit, including sharing a cell long ago. That was how they'd first met. They'd both been held in the same Scottish prison for a period of time. The place had been a hellhole. Striker had been a handful then and not much had changed.

"And how did that end for you?" asked Boomer.

James knew the answer already. "He spent a fortnight in the stockades before he finally broke free."

Striker's gaze found James. "Had me a wee bit of help."

Boomer smiled. "Dumbass."

"Och, I'm nae the *Asshole of the Week*,"

returned Striker, attempting to stand on his own merit but tipping sideways, pulling Boomer with him. "Duke is still holdin' that title good and tight."

Duke had gone bat-shit crazy when his mate had been injured during the extraction to break James free. When Duke had seen Mercy there, on the floor, partially on James's lap, bloody and not moving, he'd lost his shit and allowed the blood lust to take hold. That was a dangerous thing for a shifter to do. Some never bounced back from it. Duke had been stuck in shifter form for days—earning him the *Asshole of the Week* award.

James leaned on the stool, watching his friends, missing this type of interaction with them more than he'd thought he would. Boomer tried to go left and Striker went right, each still clinging to the other. They ended up bouncing back to the center, knocking heads.

"Bat boy, you got a hard head," said Striker, rubbing his head slightly. "Like a rock."

"Bat boy?" echoed Boomer, rubbing his head as well. "What are you talking 'bout, Scot?"

Striker pointed to the man's leather pants. Boomer seemed to have an endless wardrobe of leather. And most had silver bats on them. The pair of leather pants he currently wore were no exception. "If the leather fits."

Boomer grinned. *"I'm Batman,"* he said, throwing his voice even deeper than its normal level. "And I am kick ass."

"Yer a dumbass," offered Striker.

"I'm that too." Boomer flashed another wide smile. He put his arms out wide. "I'm Bat-Panther."

"Aye, and I'm Super-Wolf," added Striker, lifting his arms into the air and simulating flight. "I need a cape."

"Nah, your skirt should do the trick," said Boomer.

"You're *both* dumbasses." James continued to smile.

The men continued to sway and knock into one another. James took note of Boomer's t-shirt that read *Got Sparkle* and shook his head, putting it all together. "Let me guess, the Crimson Sentinels are coming in for their once-a-decade meeting with PSI Divisions."

"Och, they came last year for it," said Striker. "Blood suckers are comin' back."

"All the shit going down has the supernatural community scrambling to try to fix it," added Boomer. "My guess, they're as worried as the rest of us about it all. It affects them too."

The Fang Gang, as they'd been nicknamed over the centuries as they were all vampires, journeyed in to various PSI Division

Headquarters once every ten years for meetings. They only made visits sooner if something really bad was happening.

Coming back within a year meant the situation was dire.

Since most of PSI was made up of shifters, the vampires' arrival was always met with a healthy dose of ribbing and good intended humor on both sides. The year prior to James leaving PSI for his decade break, the Sentinels had shown up in a van marked *Dog Groomers.* They'd left gift bags on all the PSI guys' desks. Inside the bags was flea dip, dog nail clippers and pet pee pads.

Boomer ran a hand through his long, dark hair. "I got a shirt for you too. Says *Vamps Suck*. Striker got you one that says *Team Edward*. You pick which you want to wear. We'll give Tut the other if he shows."

Malik "Tut" Nasser was on forced leave.

James had yet to see Tut since James's return to PSI. While James did miss the guy and wanted to reconnect, he understood what needing to take time for one's self was like.

"Which do you want?" asked Boomer. "*Suck* or *Team Edward*?"

James shrugged, unsure what they were talking about. The only Edward he knew was a shifter out of the London division of PSI, and James wasn't about to join his team of ops. The guy was a total douchebag, all whiny and overly dramatic. The type of supernatural who led the tortured-soul kind of life because he couldn't man up and accept what he was. And the hair—the guy was always worried about it being just right. What kind of shifter worried more about his hair than he did anything else?

No thank you.

Duke Marlow, a fellow PSI-Ops and team member, entered the lab behind Striker and

Boomer. His shirt said *You are my Sunshine*. Which was actually hilarious considering how very un-sunshiny the guy was. Duke's personality ran more on the lines of crotchety old dude who looked forever locked at thirty-five but who would more than likely yell at kids to stay off his lawn. James knew Duke was only wearing the shirt to take a dig at the vampires. And if James was right, Duke's wife had pressed him to wear it.

Duke frowned at Boomer and Striker. "Aren't you two supposed to be staying in my wife's lab so she can oversee the effects of the sedative?"

"I'm doubting she could keep a handle on them," said James, turning on his stool more. "They're, and I quote, *tipsy*."

Striker and Boomer swayed together and then began to rock back and forth in place, almost as if they were dancing. Duke walked around them, ignoring them as if their behavior was commonplace. It sort of was.

Duke's onyx gaze went to James's cane. "Still need that?"

James touched the top of the cane lightly. "When I'm on my feet too long, yes. But I'm getting around without it now, for the most part."

"You should have healed by now," Duke said bluntly, never one to pull punches or beat around the bush.

"I know."

Duke neared him and glanced at the microscope. "Figure out what they fuck they did to you?"

"No," said James softly.

"Corbin asked me if you were ready for fieldwork," added Duke. "I lied and said yes, but between us, I don't think you're ready for shit."

"Tell me how you really feel," replied James. He wasn't surprised by Duke's remarks. Had Duke come in and sugarcoated everything, James would have been shocked. Hearing it spelled out by a guy he'd known a hell of a long time made sense.

Duke shrugged. "Hey, you know it's true."

James glanced over at Striker and Boomer to find they actually were dancing together now. They were waltzing through the lab as Striker started in on his William Wallace songs. James didn't comment, instead looking at his longtime friend. He knew Duke had done him a solid by lying to their captain, but James didn't think for a second Corbin really believed he was ready for full duty.

Duke took a seat on an extra stool. "Got anything in here that will blow up if those two dipshits run into it?"

James shook his head. "No. Unlike your

wife, I try to keep my testing explosions to a minimum."

"I love explosions," added Boomer from the sides of the lab.

It was how he'd gotten his nickname, so no one was surprised at his declaration.

Pride slipped over Duke's face. "My mate is a hellion and I love her."

"I know."

Duke cleared his throat. "You need to take a break from this lab and get your mind off things."

"Not really that easy," admitted James. "I need to know what's wrong with me."

"Yeah, but you haven't figured it out yet and staring at the same old shit day in and day out isn't making it any clearer. Get out of here. Relax. Do something to take your mind off it all."

James put an elbow on the counter. "As

luck would have it, I have a date tonight."

Duke's brows lifted. "With a woman?"

"No, I'm taking Dumb and Ass—" He pointed to Striker and Boomer. "—out for some quality dancing time. When we're done doing that, those two superheroes are going to single-handily save the city from evil villains."

Duke huffed. "Don't get shitty with me. It was a legit question. I know we put ten years between heart-to-hearts, but the James I remember didn't date. Hadn't actually dated in decades. He managed to get into a lot of fights, all while wearing designer clothing, but he didn't date. And let me tell you there is nothing like a smart guy, dressed to the nines, leveling a jackass."

"Jinx told me it had been over a century since I visited her place," he confessed. "I hadn't noticed it had been that long."

"Losing Elsbeth was hard on you," stated

Duke, compassion in his eyes. “She was a sweet girl, but James, she wasn’t your mate.”

He nodded, thinking back on his ex-fiancé without deep guilt consuming him as it once had. She’d died prior to them ever marrying but he had cared greatly for her. “I know. I’ve moved past her death. Really, I have, it’s just, I didn’t feel like dating.”

“Dating and fucking are not one and the same,” said Duke. He grunted. “An alpha male needs to fuck. You know it was well as I do. You could end up going off the deep end if you don’t get your rocks off and soon.”

With a shaky laugh, James shook his head. “I’m not too worried about that. I’ve managed this long without it.”

“Famous last words, brother,” whispered Duke. “Mark my words, we’ll be dealing with an out-of-control you before too long. While you may have been fine before, you’re not now.

The Corporation fucked with you, James. Who knows what will come of it. Do me a favor. Get this date of yours tonight into bed."

James bit at his lip. "You might not be hoping for that for long when I tell you more about her."

"Why? She married?" Duke questioned, judgment in his voice before he gasped. "She's not a vampire, is she?"

"No." It was amusing that Duke considered being a vampire worse than being a married woman going on a date with someone other than the man she was married to. He suspected Duke wouldn't feel the same if it was his mate they were discussing. Bet being a vampire would win out over Mercy wanting to date another man. "She is a recent person of interest to PSI, though."

Duke groaned. "Not the hacker chick. James, Corbin will shit a brick if he finds out you're romancing the target. There are millions of women out there and you go and pick the one we're looking into?"

Striker yelled from the other side of the lab. "That Bloody-English-Bastard-Out-to-Steal-My-Country can kiss my arse."

"Great, he's back on that again," murmured Duke. "Corbin will love being called that *again*."

"She's not a target," corrected James, ignoring Striker. The urge to shake Duke and make him understand that Laney was on their side—a good guy—nearly overtook him. James had to collect himself before he did something stupid like attack his own teammate.

Yep. The Corporation messed up your wiring.

"Yet," said Duke. "You don't know that she isn't a pawn in that sick place's bigger game. She could be playing you."

"She's not."

"And you know this how?" demanded Duke.

"Gut says it's the case." James leaned against the counter. "And I trust my gut. I did so with Mercy and I was right. She's good people and I knew that from the word go. The two of you are together because of it—because of my gut. All I ask is that you trust me on this. I just need to play this out more to see where it's going."

Grumbling, Duke nodded. "You're right. Fine. I'll keep a lid on this for now, but check in with me. I don't want you falling into the enemy's hands again. I fucking hate it when that happens."

"Yes, Mom," said James with a wink.

Duke eyed James's cane. "You taking that with you?"

James shook his head. "No."

"We're going drinking," announced

Boomer. "Who is in?"

"Should they drink after what Mercy gave them?" asked Duke. "I love the woman to death, but she's a menace in a lab. Did you hear about what she did yesterday?"

"I showed up right after it happened." James had to fight to keep from laughing. He had heard about Mercy's rather unfortunate experiment gone wrong. "Corbin's hair still pink?"

Duke rubbed his temples. "Yes, and the fucking Brit won't stop calling to yell at me like it's my fault he let Mercy have unlimited access to anything she wants. I told him not to be a lab rat for her. He said, *oh she's harmless*."

"Now *those* were famous last words," said James with a snort. He'd heard the explosion that had rocked the other end of the hallway at PSI the day before. When he'd gotten there, plumes of pink smoke were billowing out of

Mercy's labs. Corbin Jones had emerged, his normally blond hair shocking pink. It had taken all of James to avoid commenting. Unfortunately, Striker had been near so Corbin not only wasn't going to hear the end of it, there was now photographic proof of the incident. And knowing Striker, he'd find a way to sneak it onto the internet despite how stupid it was for an immortal to leave a photo trail.

"I fucking hate cameras," said Duke.

He hated a lot of things so James didn't comment on it. "How is Mercy doing with the pregnancy? Any morning sickness yet?"

"Nope. She is too caught up in trying to counter the Corporation's weapons and drugs. I don't think it's safe for her or the little one to be exposed to all those chemicals."

James bit his lower lip. "She's being careful."

"Our captain has pink hair," reminded

Duke.

"Probably because I took away anything dangerous and what I left her with didn't mix as planned." James shrugged. "Nothing Mercy used was harmful to her or the baby. She's careful to wear all the proper safety gear as well. Plus, she's been running her list of experiments by me. I've been double-checking. I won't let her get into anything that might be an issue."

Duke exhaled. "Thank you."

James touched Duke lightly, understanding the man was concerned for his mate and unborn babe. "Relax. She'll be fine. The baby will be fine and before you know it, you'll be a father."

Paling, Duke nodded. "I know."

"You're going to make a great dad, Duke," said James.

"You know, someday, you'll make

someone a great father too."

"I don't really see that in the stars," said James, ending the discussion on him one day mating.

"Sing with me now," said Striker loudly as he twirled Boomer in a circle. "*Oh, William, how you…*"

"Ever worry that they're our backup?" asked James, doing his best to keep from getting Striker's song stuck in his head.

The edges of Duke's mouth tilted upwards. "Every damn day."

"This would be better if your dress was a tutu," said Boomer to Striker. "You'd be like a ballerina."

Striker growled. "I'm nae wearing a dress!"

"You say tomato," mouthed Boomer, dodging a hit as he laughed.

"You guys have a weird obsession with tutus," Duke growled. "That damn monkey still wearing one?"

Boomer smiled wide. "Yes, Lil Duke, who is not a monkey, he's a chimpanzee, is still wearing a tutu."

Grumbling, Duke made underhanded comments about there being no difference between a monkey and a chimp. James had heard the entire story while he was in recovery. One of the chimps rescued from a testing lab operated by the Corporation had taken a real shine to Duke's mate. Because the chimp didn't seem to like anyone other than Mercy, she told everyone the chimp reminded her of Duke—who hates everyone. Thus, the name Lil' Duke was given to the chimp who now resided happily in an animal sanctuary that Boomer funded. And apparently Lil' Duke enjoyed playing dress up.

James lifted his head, his attention on Striker and Boomer. "If we let the two of you leave here, how much trouble are you going to get into?"

Striker held out one arm, while Boomer held out one as well. Since their other arms were now locked, holding one another up, it was a wide expanse they showed.

"This much," they said in unison.

James laughed. "That's what I thought."

"It'll be fun," said Striker. "You do remember fun, right?"

He did.

Vaguely.

"Tell you what, let's get some coffee in you and let me call Mercy to see what exactly she gave the two of you. Then, if I deem it's safe, you can leave HQ."

Boomer and Striker jumped and somehow managed to knock heads.

"I work with idiots," said James, still smiling.

"Fucking idiots," added Duke as he stood. "I'm going to collect my wife and take her home. Then I'm going to dodge any more calls from Corbin. That doesn't mean you can forget to keep me posted on your date with the hacker girl."

"Captain looks good in pink. Let's get him the tutu," said Striker. "He's gonna love the hair when he has to show for the Fang Gang meetings."

James cringed. Corbin would be impossible to be around for at least a week. Not to mention the Crimson Sentinels would not be above ribbing Corbin for the hair. After all, the rest of PSI had fun at their expense all the time.

He glanced over in time to see Boomer dipping Striker as Striker held his kilt out at an angle that looked a lot like a woman lifting her skirt.

Duke grunted. “Should I break up Ginger and Fred there?”

“I’m thinking we should record them,” added James. “Methinks we could award two *Assholes of the Weeks*.”

“I like it, but you’ll have to do the recording. I’m shit with technology.”

James laughed. Good to know some things never changed. He opened the top drawer near him and withdrew a digital camera. It had the ability to record video as well. James hit record and took a video of Boomer and Striker as they continued to dance together to the sounds of Striker singing odes to William Wallace. James took a few still shots as well. The award was always better with a picture pinned up near it for proof of the stupidity.

Duke shook his head. “I seriously cannot believe those two idiots are entrusted with million-dollar equipment, weapons and super-secret government operations."

"Or people's lives," said James.

Duke's eyes widened. "Yeah, or that."

The door to the lab opened and it took all of James to keep from laughing as the captain entered, his hair seeming even pinker than when James had last seen him.

"Captain Cotton Candy," said Striker, spinning around in a circle. He saluted Corbin, but the shit-assed grin on the man's face said he was being anything but respectful at the moment.

Corbin's unamused gaze locked onto the Scot. "Why, exactly, are you being led around the lab by Boomer as if this is a ballroom and you're the female lead?" he asked, his words clipped with a British accent.

Striker shrugged. "Och, do nae judge. Yer head is pink."

"I really wish I could fire you," returned

Corbin.

"You and the rest of PSI." Striker blew the captain a kiss. "You'd miss me. I'm special like that."

James hid his laugh. Oh, Striker was special all right.

"Want me to off him?" asked Duke, a hopeful look on his face.

Corbin rubbed his jaw as if considering the offer.

Striker grunted. "Do nae make me suggest we all take one of the jets and fly somewhere."

Duke crossed his arms over his chest in an angry protest. "I fucking hate to fly."

"We know," said the men together, snorting as they did.

Striker turned and shook his ass, holding his kilt out, lifting it to the point it just barely covered all it should. He shook his backside back and forth. "That's right. Can't get enough of the Scot love machine."

Corbin's attention went to Duke. "I'll give you a thousand dollars if you find your wife and have her shoot Striker with another tranq dart."

Duke laughed. "Ah, I'd do that for free."

James laughed. "Ask him about his milkshake."

"About his what?" questioned Corbin.

James snorted. "You probably don't want to know, sir. If I were you I'd run away while you still can before they suck you into their dance routine."

"How long before they sober up?" asked Corbin.

"Depends on how much sedatives Mercy gave them," answered James. "I'd say a couple of hours."

"Great."

"Hey, Captain Cotton Candy Head," called

Striker. "Is it nae about time for you to take a tea-and-crumpet break?" Striker and Boomer both bent forward, laughing as if Striker had said the funniest thing ever.

Corbin eyed James, looking unamused with the men's antics. James knew better. He knew that under the layer of stodgy that Corbin seemed to shroud himself in lay a man whose passions ran deep and who enjoyed the banter and playful ribbing. "Here's to hoping they sober up sooner rather than later."

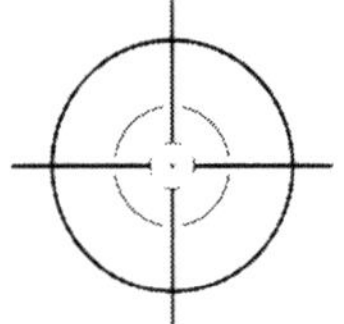

Chapter Six

The burner phone Laney had been using longer than she should rang. She should have dumped it that morning at the very latest, but she'd been too busy talking to Hagen to stop and think about it. And now she'd given him the number and didn't want to risk missing a call from him. She'd try her luck with it another day or so and then get a new one.

She picked it up and kept typing. "Yeah?"

"Nice way to answer the phone. And what in the hell are you doing? I should have gotten a text from you this morning with your new number. Why is this one still active?" asked Harmony, her voice light and airy.

"Erm, running a little behind. No worries."

Harmony huffed. "Said the girl who does nothing but worry *the Man* is watching her."

"Hey, just because I'm paranoid doesn't mean someone isn't out to get me," returned Laney with a half-laugh.

"Weirdo." Harmony blew a bubble and it popped loudly over the phone. "I thought I'd be interrupting some hot monkey phone sex with your wolf boyfriend. Have you used the toys I brought you yet?"

Laney grinned, knowing Harmony was talking about Hagen. "They're still in the boxes. I took one look and then thought, *holy moly, that is supposed to go there?"*

Harmony laughed. "It's fun. Try it."

"I'm hanging up now."

"No," said Harmony. "How is your boyfriend?"

"I barely know him and he's not my boyfriend."

She didn't believe her own words. It felt as if she'd known Hagen forever. It wasn't a connection she expected Harmony to understand. If anything, Harmony would mock it and then make light of it. As much as Laney loved the girl, she had some faults.

"I think he is. You've logged how many hours with him every night for over a week?" Harmony reminded. "I've never seen you pay any guy much mind. This one holds your attention. And, girlie, you should open the toys. They will change your life. Once you learn to be in charge of your own orgasm, the world is your oyster."

Laney snorted. "Way to channel a motivational speaker in an attempt to get me to masturbate."

"I'm a sex goddess," teased Harmony. "Do that funky thing you do. You know, the whole trance-and-spill-tidbits thing. I want to know if one day I'll be worshiped by millions of adoring men. Divine my future, oh great seer. Tell me of all the hotties I'll collect."

Laney wasn't comfortable with that side of herself—the trance bit—as Harmony liked to call it. The side that scared her. She never felt in control of herself and she certainly couldn't do it on command. The first time it had happened in front of Harmony, Laney thought it would be the end of their friendship. That Harmony wouldn't want to hang out with the freak who said weird, cryptic things at random times.

Harmony had given her an odd look

before smiling wide and informing her that they needed to get her a crystal ball and some tarot cards.

Stat.

"I don't think we need me to divine anything. My guess, it will be a broken-hearts club they're joining in regards to you."

Harmony laughed.

"You're going to be proud of me. I have a date with him tonight. It's just coffee, but still," said Laney, her shoulders going back as her posture straightened.

Harmony squealed. "Yay! Ohmygod, my girlie has a date. A real, live date. I'm so proud. I've taught you well. You going to sleep with him?"

Laney processed all of what Harmony had rattled off at such a fast pace, and without a breath, that Laney still wasn't sure how the girl did it. As she put together what she'd been asked, she sucked in a big breath. "What? No!"

"Lighten up. I was joking," said Harmony with the same attitude she had about most things. "I'm just happy you're going to shower and get out of that hacking cave. I bet you're starting to smell. Have computer wires grown up and around you like spider webs, trying to reclaim you—their mothership of weird?"

"Eat me and my mothership," said Laney.

"I'll leave that for LabLupus," teased Harmony, a suggestive note hanging in the air. "Or you could try out the toys I brought you."

"Horn ball."

"Thanks. Oh, and here are some valuable dating tips from an expert. Dress less *Laney* and be less conspiracy theorist, okay? He's a doctor. Impress him. Don't scare him with your talk of secret government agencies. Save that for date two."

"He already knows about my radical

ideas," Laney returned. She entertained hanging up on her friend, but that would only prompt Harmony to show up on her doorstep. Harmony hated where Laney lived and the fact that the building was filled with what Harmony thought were vagabonds. "And I don't think he cares what I wear."

Harmony ignored her. "Wear that black mini skirt you have and that cute off-the-shoulder matching top."

"The fact that you memorize my wardrobe is really weird," added Laney, still typing, adding a few more lines to her post-in-progress. It would open the world's eyes to what was really going on. Or, at the very least, make them think and wonder.

She couldn't ask for more.

Harmony grunted. "You barely own any clothes, so it doesn't take long."

Fair point.

Laney grinned.

"Call me when you get to the coffee shop and text me several times so I know he didn't murder you or anything," said Harmony, a certain parental tone evident. "If you vanish, I'm going to have to publish that folder you keep—the *in the event of my death* one."

"My folder is a brilliant idea," challenged Laney. "Should *the Man* actually get me, everyone should know the truth. You remember where my backup system is, right?"

"Well, you only show me and remind me of it monthly. Someday, I'm going to meet this *man* you're so against and I'm going to kick him in the nuts just for making me hear about him for so long. Until then, I'll let you run with your bag of crazy because you're my sista from another mother."

"Gee, thanks," said Laney.

"What are friends for?" Harmony was

quiet a moment. “Hey, random thought, but what if wolf guy is really working for the same people you’re trying to track down information on? What if he is tricking you into a meeting to cut you up in little pieces?”

“Thanks for the awesome show of support. And thanks for freaking me the hell out before I get ready for my first date.” Laney shook off the unease Harmony’s question had brought about. There was no way Hagen was part of what she was investigating. She trusted him.

“I’m a stone-cold, back-up bitch,” said Harmony. “Keep me on speed dial and my ass will be showing up there with the police in tow. They’d come marching in, guns a-blazing, ready to protect my girlie girl.”

“Uh, not them. Not the police. They’re part of the establishment,” said Laney. “I’ll be fine. He’s a good guy. I have a great feeling about him.”

"Like a great enough feeling to want him to make your Va-jay-jay quiver with delight?" asked Harmony with a laugh. "He could totally talk dirty to you by just explaining his computer set up. You'd be moaning, groaning, thinking of ways to trick it out. Bling his system. Uh oh, talk syntax to me, baby."

Laney paused, her full attention going to the conversation. She wasn't really sure how to be a sex kitten, and the idea of embarrassing herself with a guy like Hagen didn't sit well with her. "You don't think he's going to expect me to sleep with him on the first date, do you?"

"He's male," answered Harmon flatly. "Besides, we need to get your V-card punched, girlie." Harmony laughed. "You're twenty-two and a virgin. That isn't weird to you? It freaks me the hell out."

"No. I happen to like my V-card intact,"

returned Laney, sitting back in her chair. The dim, pale greenish-colored lighting in her computer room made her skin appear even paler than it was. "And I'm not about to hand it to just anyone."

Though Hagen isn't just anyone.

Harmony snorted. "So, no hanging chads on your V-card?"

"If anyone has anything hanging I shouldn't see, I'm gonna be sick." With a groan, Laney touched her desktop. Her friend was something else. But in all honestly, the idea of Hagen's man bits did sort of excite her. "For realz, Harm."

"For *real-zy*," Harmony returned. "And let's be honest, LabLupus could be a hot stud and you could find yourself begging him to do you."

"Bitch."

"You know it," she added with a laugh. "If

the Fates feel the need to throw a hottie your way, you should take him. Though, at this point, I'm thinking you've fallen off the Fates' radar. I think you might be in the giant bin of lost causes. Probably why they made our paths cross. I'm there too, but for other digressions."

She had a way of objectifying men that made Laney blush, even when she was alone in her workspace. "Love ya like a sister, but you are a real piece of work."

"Well, it gives me something to do. Life is hard," said Harmony.

"Oh yeah," joked Laney. "Up in the mansion with how many sports cars and staff? Tell me again, how many maids cleaned your room this morning?"

Harmony clucked her tongue. "I cannot help my father is loaded. He spends money like it grows on trees."

"I know. I think you slum it with me to

spite him," added Laney. There was truth to her words. She had a feeling that in the beginning that was exactly what Harmony did. The friendship became real and their shared love of hacking cemented a bond between them that had only strengthened over the years, despite their differences.

"Daddy doesn't know we're friends. You made me swear not to tell anyone. Freak."

"You know it. Gotta stay off *the Man's* radar," said Laney. "Big Brother is always watching."

"Oh, let's give him a show. We could wear sexy nighties and rub each other with lotion. I bet that will turn him on."

Laney groaned. "Not funny. You don't want to be on their radar, Harmony. You don't want them watching you and looking into every aspect of your life."

Well, before you break out the tinfoil hat

—"

"Don't joke about it," said Laney sternly.

"Okay, okay, but can you come let me in before— Ugh. Never mind."

"Wait, you're here?" asked Laney.

"Yes, and Captain Black has found me," said Harmony, the line going dead.

Laney laughed and hung up the phone. Whenever Harmony grew brave enough to stop by unannounced, she normally had to deal with Casey, or Captain Black as Harmony liked to call him because of all his facial hair and long, black hair. The proper thing to do as a friend was to go down to the lowest floor of the old hotel, which no longer was operating as such, and meet Harmony. The funnier option was to let Casey escort her.

Casey was a mystery to Laney, but she cared for him as if he were family. He had certain fatherly aspects about him, but he wasn't nearly old enough to have fathered her. She wasn't exactly sure of his age because he hid behind a lot of facial hair, but she thought he was probably in his late twenties, early thirties.

He, like the rest of the men she often referred to as her boys, lived in the old hotel with her. Casey seemed as if he could function on his own in the real world, unlike the others, but he didn't leave much that she knew of. He was a recluse of sorts.

"Get your hands off me." Harmony's voice filtered through the halls.

"Keep walking, blondie," said a gruff voice. "And stop shaking your backside at me or I'm going to spank it."

"I'll bite you," Harmony responded.

"I like a little pain with my sex."

Harmony snorted. "Me too, Captain Black."

Laughing, Laney stood and headed out of her computer cave to meet Harmony at the door. The place wasn't much. At one point it had been a fancy room with a small kitchen and two bedrooms. Years and neglect had left it looking a little worse for wear, but it was home. She and the others lived rent and utilities free because of her hacking skills.

She made it to the door and opened it in time to see a perky blonde trying, but failing, to get her elbow free from a man with tousled black hair and a beard that was so long and scruffy that it was hard to make out much of his face. He wore a seventies rock band t-shirt that was threadbare and had a few holes in it. Harmony had on designer clothing from head to toe.

Such a contrast in her two friends.

Casey held Harmony by the arm as he led her to Laney's door. "Did you lose this?"

Laney snorted. "No, but thanks for bringing her up. She tends to freak out when the other guys say hello to her."

"One of them still thinks he's in Vietnam," said Harmony quickly. "He's always trying to get me to duck and cover right before he asks me if I want a hit of acid. And that other one, he just stares all weird at me."

Laney sighed. "Gus stares at everyone. It's what he does. He's a gentle soul but he doesn't speak. That doesn't mean he's dangerous."

Casey grunted. "And it's not Bill's fault that he often thinks he's back in Nam. It's all the shit the government did to him back then. Fucking LSD experiments. You really have no idea how much the government has done on people, testing-wise, on people without the world knowing."

Harmony rolled her eyes and gave Laney a pointed stare. "You're a freaky conspiracy theorist because you live with a bunch of them."

"Like attracts like," replied Laney with a smile. "Thanks for bringing her up, Casey."

"You can stop touching me now, Neanderthal," snapped Harmony.

Casey kept hold of her. "Say please, Princess."

Harmony growled and it sounded ridiculous. Even Casey cracked a smile, something he didn't do too often.

"You're infuriating," said Harmony, though her voice lacked malice.

"And you're a fucking ray of sunshine," Casey shot back. He released Harmony and she made quite the production of rubbing her elbow. Laney knew Casey hadn't harmed her friend. Harmony had a flare for the dramatics. He looked to Laney. "We're still on for a session, right?"

Laney bit her inner cheek, forgetting she'd agreed to another self-defense training lesson from Casey. He was very big on her learning to handle herself. She wasn't sure why. All she did know was when she'd started nosing around and asking him questions about the stories he'd once told her—of men who could shift into animals—he'd started making her meet him weekly for sessions. "Well, I need to reschedule."

He lifted a brow.

Harmony plastered a smile to her face, her blue eyes dancing with delight. She shook her chest a bit and swayed her hips. "Our little girlie here has a date tonight."

Casey's face went blank—totally unreadable. "With?"

"A guy she met on the internet," replied Harmony, not helping the situation any.

Laney could feel the disapproval leaking

off Casey. He locked gazes with her, dark brown eyes holding concern. "Is that wise?"

"No," said Harmony. "But look at her. She's a social leper. If she doesn't meet a man online, she'll never meet one."

Laney put her hands on her hips. "Really, you two. I'll be fine. He's very sweet and a gentleman and he's funny. We're meeting for coffee. Somewhere public."

"Laney," Casey said, his voice even. "What have I told you again and again?"

She groaned. "Don't trust anyone. Ever."

"Wow. You guys are like total freaks," said Harmony, shoving at Casey but not budging him. "Go. I have to help her get ready for her date and you're in the way."

He stared at her and looked her over slowly. "How did the two of you end up friends?"

"She needed style sense," said Harmony.

Laney grinned. "And she needed to know how to boost a car."

Casey shook his head as he left Laney's place. Harmony shut the door behind him and then put her back to it, sighing loudly. "Why does he have to be such a jerkwad and so yummy?"

Harmony thought Casey was yummy?

Laney didn't respond. "Okay, spill it. Why are you really here?"

Harmony paused and the silence was awkward, considering how much Harmony loved to hear her own voice at times. "Can we meet tomorrow? I don't want to get into it tonight with you heading out on a date and all. There are some odd things I've noticed around my house that I just want to bounce off someone. You can then spin them out of proportion and make me feel better."

"I can cancel." She didn't want to but she

would. Her friendship was important to her.

Harmony's eyes widened. "You will not do anything of the sort. You're gonna go shake your moneymaker."

"My what?"

Harmony pushed on her. "Let's get you showered and see if we can make you presentable."

"Gee, the love just pours off you."

Harmony smiled. "We'll meet up tomorrow, right?"

"Of course. We'll meet for breakfast at *Stew's Diner*."

"If you don't show, I'll assume you're a statistic," reminded Harmony before she practically shoved Laney into the bathroom. "And no one wants to be a statistic.

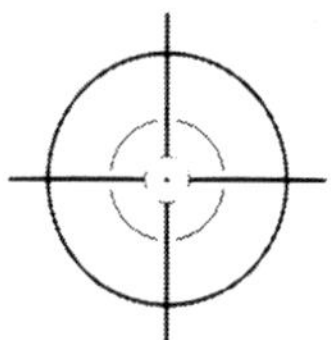

Chapter Seven

James stood outside the small, neighborhood coffee shop. It was lit to a point one could see all the customers within through the windows this time of night. Most customers were on varying electronic devices, paying little mind to one another. He couldn't help but reflect on how much the world had changed since he'd been alive. There used to be people having conversations with one another in person.

Not anymore.

Everyone had their noses in something that plugged in.

He leaned against a lamppost, his leg throbbing from the burn of standing so long. Nervous he'd somehow miss out on meeting Laney face-to-face, he'd arrived nearly an hour early. He'd showered, shaved and changed at work in the bathroom off his office, installed in the event James pulled an all-nighter, which he'd been known to do a lot in the past and old habits did indeed die-hard.

A group of women approached. They were walking so close together he wondered how they didn't trip over one another. A stacked blonde left the group and stepped in his direction. She had full lips and actually made a kissy face at him, batting her long lashes.

"What are you doing out here all alone?"

James put his hands in his pockets and took a small step away from her. She wasn't Laney. He knew by her voice and his gut instincts that this was not the woman he was meeting tonight.

The woman who blew him the kiss wasn't bad on the eyes at all. Some would say she was hot. And she was what he normally went for, but the shiny had worn off what he used to want. All he wanted now was for his little hacker to arrive. He didn't care what she looked like.

"Waiting for my date," he said with a slight incline of his head.

"She stand you up?" asked the woman, her friends forming a half circle behind her, looking a lot like a posse in Prada.

James grinned. "No. I got here an hour early. I didn't want her to think I was standing her up."

The woman eyed him and then shook her head. "You've got it bad for her, huh?"

"I think so," he said. He knew he had it *bad*. Admitting it was half the battle.

Her friends laughed and she waved a hand in the air. "Any man who arrives an hour early for a date has it bad for the girl."

James knew she was right. He merely shrugged, giving a sheepish grin. It was against his manly code to offer anything more. That was enough. It said what he wouldn't.

The woman winked as if she fully understood where he was coming from. "Good luck. I hope she's worth it."

"She is," he said with conviction.

The women walked away and James began to obsess about his appearance once more. He wasn't even sure what to wear on a date, he'd not been on one in so long. Boomer had gone with him a week after his return to work to replenish his wardrobe. James had decided to keep a portion of it at the office. He spent most of his time there rather than his home—a place that had been handed to him along with his position. He had enough money to buy his own place. PSI paid ridiculously well. So much so that he could have stopped working centuries ago.

When he had more time, he'd get some more relaxed articles of clothing. Currently he only owned two pairs of jeans and two t-shirts, not counting the *Team Edward* one he'd grabbed to shut Boomer up. Though, he'd left the shirt on his desk.

James had decided on black dress pants, black boots because he felt comfortable in them, and a blue, silk dress shirt. Duke had tried to talk him into jeans. He'd refused. Now he wasn't sure he'd made the right choice. He continued to fidget with his shirt, wondering if he should have gone with a t-shirt and jeans, if this get-up was too much for coffee.

James took out his phone and texted the number Laney had given him. *Having a wardrobe rethink. I feel like a teenage boy. You should get here soon so you can save me from myself. LabLupus.*

He laughed partially under his breath. "Oh, how the mighty alpha male has fallen."

He was about to text more when he sensed something. At first, he wasn't sure what it was, only that it commanded his attention, drawing it from his text in the other direction. It took James several long seconds to realize what it was he was sensing.

A woman.

Not just any woman either.

One he *had* to see like he had to draw in air.

Breathe, he told himself, and then finally

listened and did just that.

His entire body strummed with the feel of her approaching. His hands tingled and he lifted them, looking down at them, wondering what in the hell was going on. Every fiber of his being seemed to come to life, his gaze moving slowly towards the end of the street. There, across the way, was the young woman from his vision. Her long dark hair with purple streaks was pulled into a high ponytail. Her chocolate gaze was mesmerizing. She looked down at a phone in her hand.

His wolf, who had been missing in action for months, picked then to prickle to life, waking slowly. He felt it nosing around within him, wondering what this new curiosity was.

Was it food?

No, he and the wolf found a quick understanding. The woman was not prey.

Far from it.

The wolf pushed up more, wanting free, wanting to investigate the woman. James gasped and touched his chest, the biting pain in his leg lessening somewhat as he stared, totally enamored, with the female across the street from him.

She smiled and James nearly lost his footing. When she laughed at whatever it was she was reading on her cell phone, James's cock hardened. This was not the time or place for that.

She's in danger.

He'd sensed it and seen it for himself in his vision. His cock didn't seem to compute the severity of the situation because it hardened more. It wanted in the woman and the wolf was in total agreement with his cock.

Ganging up on me. Great.

The woman, decked out in dark attire, was not what he'd normally find attractive. He tended to like his women refined, dressed in high-end clothing, and to have an air of elegance about them.

However she's dressed and whatever her hair looks like, she will be beautiful.

Guilt crept over him as he thought about Laney and the fact that he was meeting her soon. He'd established a deep connection with her and here he was panting over a stranger.

This wasn't like him.

He didn't collect women. He wasn't Striker or Boomer. For fuck's sake, he'd had one serious relationship in his life. Elsbeth had been a shifter as well and her death had shaken him greatly. He'd known she wasn't his mate, that they could never truly be bonded. Yet, he'd been loyal to her even far beyond her passing.

He couldn't help but look back at the girl from his vision. He was drawn to her in a way he'd never been drawn to Elsbeth. The only other woman he'd experienced anything similar with was Laney. Their conversations were like drugs to him—he couldn't kick the habit.

He didn't even want to.

The woman from his vision approached the coffee shop he was to meet Laney at and then entered. When she was just inside the door he saw her texting.

His cell phone buzzed and he pulled it from his pocket. He read the —*Unless you're in a clown suit, I'm guessing you're perfect. If you are, in fact, in a clown suit, I might bail. They freak me out.*

James looked from his phone to the woman who had just entered the coffee shop. The woman who was on her phone, smiling. It couldn't be.

No.

He dialed her number, needing to know. The phone rang and James watched, a rush of adrenaline spiking through him, as the woman in the shop with the purple streaks in her hair lifted her phone, putting it to her ear.

"Hey, sexy, which one are you? I'm in here, and don't take this the wrong way, but there are nothing but hipsters hanging in here. Are you a hipster?" she asked, turning, facing him. "Say it ain't so. I have standards. I'd rather date a clown."

James watched her mouth move, syncing up to the words he was hearing. As he put it all together, fear raced over him. He'd had the vision of her being in danger and he had a deep connection with her.

"You there?" she asked.

James took a step forward, and the moment his booted foot touched the street, his sensitive hearing returned tenfold, taking him to his knees. He twisted, dropped his phone and covered his ears as the sounds of the city crashed into him. Through the fog of it all he heard the distinct sound of squealing tires and smelled exhaust fumes.

He blinked open his eyes open, his hands still on his head as he turned just enough to see two large black vans speeding in his direction. For a moment, he could do nothing, realizing who they were—the Corporation. They were just like the vans that had come when he'd been ambushed and taken prisoner. Just like the ones that had changed his life, and they were back. It would have been so easy to permit the panic welling to overtake him.

But something tugged at his gut, forcing his gaze to Laney, who was standing at the door of the cafe, about to head out, her phone pressed to her ear, confusion on her beautiful face.

He heard it then—her voice coming from his cell phone on the street. "Hagen? Hagen, are you there? What's wrong? Something is wrong. I can *feel* it."

She stepped out of the cafe and her gaze whipped across the street to him. He shook his head as the vans came closer. The realization hit him that they weren't there for him. They were there for Laney.

No, his beast roared from within.

"Laney, run!" he shouted.

She froze in place, looking stunned, her phone moving from her ear as she stared across the street at him. "Hagen? Ohmygod, what's wrong?"

She didn't run from the area. Instead, the crazy fool of a woman ran at him. He forced himself to his feet and pulled his hands from his head. "Go! Run!"

She kept coming, hitting the midway point

of the street just as the vans lined up with her. They weren't going to stop. They were going to run her down. Something snapped inside him.

She was not to be harmed.

With a speed that shocked even him, James shot forward, going at her head-on. He wrapped his arms around her gently, the sweet smell of her filling his head as he swept her up and off her feet, racing forward with her in the direction of the coffee shop. The racing vans buzzed right past him, exactly where she'd been standing, before they screeched to a halt.

James didn't stop. He kept running, right past the coffee shop. He darted into a side alley with her. Raced down it, reaching out with his senses, hoping they wouldn't fail him.

The telltale sound of weapons being prepped for firing reached him. Whatever the Corporation had done had left his abilities and his wolf feeling supercharged and out of control. He couldn't worry on that now. His only concern was Laney.

Twisting, he pushed her body against an alcove in the building, using his own body to shield hers as bullets whipped past them. One grazed his shoulder, the bite of it stinging slightly. Within seconds the sensation was gone, his body hopped up on adrenaline and testosterone.

His senses on overdrive, he zeroed in on the enemy's location. With one hand and countless years' worth of muscle memory he grabbed for his ankle holster and realized he wasn't wearing his weapon. It was in his car, which was parked across the street from the coffee shop. He'd not wanted to scare the shit out of Laney by packing heat. He didn't want her running screaming from him thinking he'd arranged a face-to-face with her, only to bring a weapon.

Fuck.

James reached out via the mental pathway he'd established with his teammates long ago. One he'd not used in over ten years. He wasn't even sure it would still work. Normally, Striker would have been the teammate he connected with first because of their long-standing bond. But at last check Striker was still coming down from the Mercy-Juice, and James couldn't risk the message going astray.

Duke.

There was a tingling and then familiar energy pressed over him.

James? responded Duke.

We're taking fire.

Who is we? asked Duke.

My date and me.

Son-of-a-bitch! I knew this was a bad idea. I knew that hacker was trouble. Where are you?

Mugs coffee shop. Alley next to it," he pushed

out with his mind, his body on fire and his wolf wanting free, wanting to be let out and allowed to kill all those who had threatened their woman. *I'm unarmed and unable to shift.*

On it, returned Duke. *Stay safe, brother.*

What is your ETA?

Duke's silence hit James like a ton of bricks. He knew Duke had left PSI headquarters to take Mercy home and get her settled in for the night. He also knew that Corbin had left as well, with Boomer and Striker, intent on making sure they went home and not out on the town, since they weren't totally free from the aftereffects of the Mercy-Juice.

Shit.

We'll be there as fast as we can, brother. Do whatever you have to do in order to survive, pushed Duke.

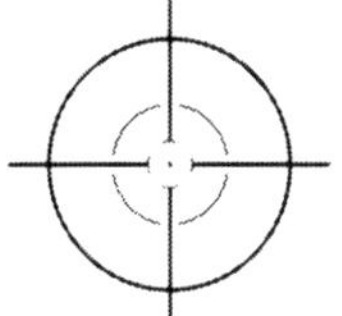

Chapter Eight

The connection slammed closed on James as the smell of gunfire, sweat and adrenaline filled the air, but the scent of death crept over it as well. The men had killed someone.

Probably an innocent bystander.

The authorities had more than likely already been called by others who heard the commotion. His teammates would know that

—they would know to intercept the calls and to assure the responding officers were supernatural, not human.

It was amazing the number of supernatural-related crimes that happened in the world daily that were covered up so humans wouldn't learn the truth of it all. They'd never handle knowing there was bigger and badder shit out there than them.

James was so focused on the bad guys that he didn't notice the screams at first. When he was able to draw into himself enough to realize who they were coming from, he paused, his gaze moving to Laney.

She screamed again, trying to get away from him, but he didn't understand why. He'd just saved her life. And he certainly wasn't the one who tried to run her down with a van before using her as target practice. That was the other guys.

"Laney, stop. It's me. I won't hurt you," he said, trying to keep his voice low and reassuring without drawing the attention of the men down the alleyway. They were busy taking turns popping off shots.

Laney's brown eyes were wide with fright as she stared at his arms. What the hell would scare her about his arms? James glanced down and froze. He was partially shifted—long, dark fur coating his now larger arms. Clawed hands held Laney pinned to the wall.

Shit!

He'd not cut her, thank the gods. He tried to force himself to shift back but couldn't. Not with the bullets still buzzing by. Whatever had been done to him had changed his makeup enough that he was basically learning what it was to live with his wolf all over again. Like it had been when he'd gone through puberty and the first full shifts had occurred. His pack wasn't exactly big on caring or sharing so he suffered through it alone.

He locked gazes with Laney, trying to convey with his expression how connected he felt to her. How protective he felt. How much she meant to him and that he was safe to be around.

Claim her.

Okay, maybe convey to her that he was mostly safe to be around. Setting aside his body having lost its ability to rationalize who was and wasn't his mate. It certainly didn't help any that she smelled like heaven to him. That only confused his senses more.

Not that they needed much help.

"I swear. I can explain. I'm not the one trying to hurt you. The guys with guns are."

She stopped screaming and with shocked, wide eyes, looked up at him, her bottom lip trembling. Confusion covered her beautiful face and she tugged at her ear. "Guys with guns?"

James would have found humor at the absurdity of her missing the detail that they were being shot at, but it wasn't the time or place for that. "Yes, sweeting, guys with guns."

Her attention went to the end of the alley where the gunfire was coming from. Several more shots went off, making her jolt beneath his touch. Her mouth formed an "O" right before her forehead crinkled in question. "Why do they have guns and why are they trying to kill us?"

James swallowed hard, the knowledge of it all settling into his bones. The Corporation had sent a hit team after her. He wasn't sure how they'd found her or how they'd known what she looked like when, according to the information PSI had, the Corporation had only expressed a limited interest in her.

His gut clenched.

Thoughts of traitors in PSI hit him hard. Had they altered the information PSI had received on the Corporation? Had they left out certain details? Or was something or someone else at play in this?

Whatever was going on, the Corporation wasn't messing around. They wanted her dead. That meant she'd hit pay dirt with her data mining on the Corporation. "Not *us*, Laney. You."

She tensed. "Me?"

He nodded.

She exhaled slowly. "It's because of my research, isn't it?"

"Yes." There was no reason to continue to lie to her. She needed to hear the truth. Needed to hear why she was being hunted.

She trembled and moisture welled in her eyes. If she dared to cry he wasn't sure what he'd do—or what his wolf would decide it would do. He had a feeling it would involve totally and completely wolfing out and probably going on a killing spree—much the same way Duke had weeks prior when he thought his mate was dead. No one wanted that. And covering up a rabid werewolf tearing through the city streets leaving a wake of bodies in its trail would be a tall order even for the skilled cleaners PSI possessed.

She clutched his arms, her fingers caressing his fur. His muscles tensed beneath the weight of her touch. "And you're not human, are you?"

"No, but I won't hurt you," he said quickly, realizing just how small she was in comparison to him. She came to his shoulder at best. He had to seem imposing to her, not to mention he was partially shifted. That would scare the ever-loving shit out of just about anyone who wasn't aware shifters were real. "I swear to you."

She put her palm to his chest and he waited to feel her start to push him away. She didn't. Some of his anxiety eased. The notion that she might reject him had gnawed at his gut. He wouldn't handle her turning away from him and shutting him out of her life. He'd bounced back from other losses, some quite serious, but a part of him knew down deep—soul deep—he'd not come out the other side in one piece if this woman rejected him. The sureness of that knowledge puzzled him.

Whatever had been done to James during his time in captivity left his head a mess and his body responding to someone it shouldn't. He was acting like Laney was his mate. She was human. Humans weren't mate material.

Period.

The gunfire ended and James heard the

men's footfalls as they stepped into the alley. One stepped on broken glass, and the sound of it crunching beneath the sole of the man's shoe seemed to be jacked up to eleven on James's hearing scale. He'd feared long-term hearing loss because of the tortures he'd endured. One device in particular had been extra damaging to his ears. It was some sort of an ultrasonic wave emitter. The noise from it couldn't be heard by a human, but to an animal or a supernatural it was ear splitting and could cause deafness.

Now his hearing not only seemed to be back, it was back with a vengeance. He could even hear the shallow breaths the men were taking.

"You see them?" asked one with a distinct Jersey accent to his voice.

"I can't see shit back here," replied another in nothing more than a whisper, yet James heard it as plain as day. “Think we got the bitch?”

My woman is not a bitch.

He nearly lost his cool and rushed out of their hiding place just to have it out with the thug for daring to say such a thing. He wisely thought better of it. He’d be of no use to Laney riddled with bullets, and with how slow he’d been to heal injuries since being tortured, he’d probably bleed out and die before he could get her to safety.

Not that he cared about himself. His only worry was her. He would gladly give himself for her safety.

She’s mine.

Laney’s fingers kneaded at James’s shirt as she pressed herself closer to him, despite him being in partially shifted form. She was accepting him. The comprehension eased over him, rejuvenating him. His cock perked and he nearly groaned at how much it seemed to not care about their circumstances. All it wanted to do was find its way into the sexy woman before him. It didn't give a rat's ass that they were in danger. And he had zero control of it. Apparently, it had a mind of its own and an iron will.

"Ah fuck, they're gone," said Jersey, his voice even closer than before. "They must have slipped into that other building. Let's go search it."

"Why didn't he tell us the man would be with her?" asked the other.

James turned his head slightly, listening, waiting to strike if they moved any closer. He'd not permit Laney to be harmed. He didn't care who he had to kill to protect her. She was his.

His?

What? Why the hell do I keep saying that?

Whatever they'd done to him must have

been a doozey.

"I don't know, but the boss is gonna wanna hear about it. He was right. The guy protected her," stated Jersey. "Call for backup. A team isn't far from here. They can splinter off and send some of those fucking freak things to help track these two."

By *freak things* James knew the man was talking about the hybrid mercenaries the Corporation was creating to fight its own private war. James had his first run in with them the night he'd been captured by the Corporation. He'd lasted nearly an hour, fighting alone against fifteen of the Pet Projects, as he liked to call them, before he'd finally succumbed.

It had been one hell of a fight.

"Bertrand is going to flip his lid," said the other.

The mention of the name Bertrand set

James on edge. The scientist had been the leader of the torture bandwagon when James had been locked up in Donavon Dynamics' holding facility in France. Bertrand was a sick bastard. The type of person who derived great pleasure out of another's pain. The kind of guy who got off on it and his ability to try to exert power over another. James would see Bertrand dead soon enough. He'd pledged that to himself months ago.

Get revenge later. Protect Laney now.

"Let's go," stated Jersey.

James waited until they were long gone from hearing range before he stepped back, releasing Laney, and even then it was only with reluctance that he let her go. He had to struggle with himself to keep from laying claim to her then and there—to make his mark on her so all knew she was under his protection. That she belonged to him.

She's not yours. Your head is fucked up. Now, step back more from the sexy little goth gal. The more distance the better. He sighed. *What the fuck is she wearing? It smells fantastic…*

His willpower sucked. He could only hope Laney had better sense than he did. He fully expected her to run from him. He wouldn't blame her. It wasn't everyday a young woman found herself pinned to a wall by a wolf shifter while people shot at her.

She didn't run.

She didn't even budge.

Shit. Her common sense was gone too.

She simply stared at him, her gaze moving up and down him slowly, seeming to soak in the sight of him. With a hesitant movement, she stepped forward in his direction. "Does that hurt?"

He lifted a brow, not quite following what she was asking about.

She pointed to his arms. "That."

He let out a small snort, thinking about being able to shift once more, even if only partially. "No. Feels good to be able to do it again. Thought I might never be able to." The fact he'd only partially shifted and without even realizing he'd done as much was worrisome. Green's words echoed in James's head. What if he was now more than he'd been before? What if 'more than' meant if James did fully shift, he'd lose total control of himself and end up trapped as some mindless killing machine?

A crazed alpha werewolf on the warpath?

Her hand found his arm and she touched it lightly, running her hand over it. "LabLupus." She shook her head in disbelief before a half-laugh fell free from her. "Doc Wolf was spot on, wasn't it?"

He nodded, afraid to move or speak too

much and scare her away. She had nailed it when she'd given him the nickname. He let her touch him, each swipe of her hand making need pulse through him. She continued to unintentionally tease him with her tender touch. He had to bite back a groan as she slinked her hands down his torso, nearing his groin. If she went any further she'd have her hand on his cock.

Oh gods above, yes please.

She stopped just shy of his groin.

Dammit.

Her scent drove him mad. Whatever perfume she was wearing was messing with his head and throwing his sex drive into overdrive. He tried to focus on anything but wanting to fuck her against the building.

Didn't work.

If anything, it only made him want to fuck her more.

Dammit, get a hold of yourself.

He was acting like Striker. The next he knew he'd be dancing around the alley, singing his own songs to fallen Scottish lycan legends. Worse yet, he'd want to wear a kilt and post pictures of himself online all day.

He flinched.

No thanks.

Laney kept her eye on his arms. "Is it catching?"

"Only if I decided to maul you to near death and exchanged blood with you and your body didn't reject the change," he said before thinking better of it.

"*Only* if all that?" she asked, her eyes wide.

He grunted. "Yes."

She puckered her lips. "Think you can resist doing that?"

He scratched the back of his head nervously. While he wanted to tell her yes, he wasn't entirely sure he trusted himself enough to commit to yes. "Probably."

"Probably?" Her brows raised.

He shrugged. "Okay, yes."

"Good because that would seriously blow," she said. "And it would really add a ton of time to shaving my legs each morning."

He grinned.

Her smile back seemed somewhat shaky, reserved even, as if she was barely clinging to the ability to keep a brave face. His chest ached for her as she stepped even closer to him and then surprised him by easing her arms around his waist and plastering herself to him, hugging him. She continued to shake and he wrapped his arms around her, mindful of his clawed hands. Holding her felt right.

Natural.

As if she'd been made to be held by him.

She trembled in his arms and he rocked her

back and forth gently, his lips finding the top of her head. He kissed her head. As he tried to soothe her, James found his arms returning to normal. Once he was in full man form again, he brought his hands up and held her tighter to him. "Shh, sweeting, I've got you. I won't let them hurt you."

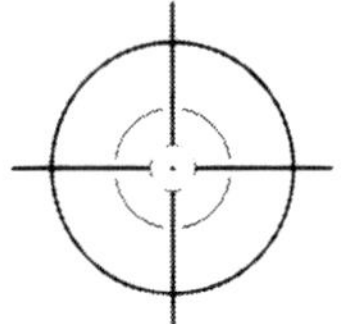

Chapter Nine

Laney felt as if she were trying to glue herself to the man before her. He rubbed her back lightly, and the feel of his powerful body against her somehow chased away some of the fear and confusion. She put her forehead to his hard, chiseled chest.

Sweet Virginal Goddess, the man is ripped.

She nearly put her hands to his chest just

to pet him and feel his muscles under her fingertips too. While she refrained from going to that extreme, she did sort of rub her face on his chest somewhat, enjoying the feel of his hard body. She wasn't exactly exposed to a lot of hunky males—aside from Casey, who Harmony thought was something, but Laney just didn't see it.

The guy was certainly in shape. She knew because he sometimes instructed her on self-defense minus a shirt, but nothing about his manly body made her hormones react the way they were to Hagen.

Ohmygod, my hormones are paranormal junkies. Just like me.

Another thought occurred to her.

She'd spent so long trying to prove the existence of the supernatural, and here she was hugging one. Heck, she'd been talking to one all week and even agreed to a coffee date, never understanding he'd been right under her nose. Only she could miss the obvious, so used to having to dig through piles upon piles of coding that she wasn't used to answers being out in the open. She burst into a fit of the giggles and eased back from his hold. "I'm being held by a werewolf."

He seemed cautious at first, his emerald-green gaze holding concern. Then he smiled and Laney's breath caught. She'd been right about him. He was gorgeous. "I told you that you were sexy. Make note, I was right. Score for me."

He's also not human.

That right there should have sent her running from him. Yet, she couldn't fathom the idea of being away from him. She slipped her hands into his and moved her lips to the side, giving him a silly face. "Bet you didn't think your date tonight would have purple streaks in her hair, did ya?"

Hagen flashed an even wider smile as he squeezed her hands gently. "Nope. Total shocker."

"Yeah, I'm full of surprises like that," she said, before looking at the building next to them. "Should we leave now?"

"In a second. They're looking out the window on the fifth floor, checking the alley. They can't see us right now—we're pressed into the darkened area too far," he said.

She blinked up at him. "Do I want to know how it is you know that?"

A sheepish grin spilled over his face. "I can hear them talking and smell them from here."

"Neat," she returned. "Any other cool party tricks?"

He lowered his head, his full lips quirking. "A few. How about you?"

"Well, I can't sport my own fur coat, if that

is what you're asking," she returned, her heart finally settling. She'd felt like it might actually burst free from her chest for a few minutes there. "And I can't hear people talking five floors up or down the alley. You're going to end this date because I'm lacking, aren't you?"

"Gods no," he said, his head lowering more, his lips so very close.

Laney had to tear her gaze from them. "Um, should we go now?"

"Probably, but I'm having a hard time convincing myself to move from this spot," said Hagen. "I really want to kiss you."

"Oh." Her eyes widened. "Oh!"

"Yes, oh," he said, his lips crashing down on hers.

Laney's hands went to his chest and she stilled, the feel of his tongue easing over hers taking all her thoughts from her.

It was just her.

Just Hagen.

Just kissing.

And, oh boy, could the man kiss.

Laney rocked on the balls of her feet before going to her tiptoes to increase their kissing heat level. Hagen smiled against her lips and then began to kiss her more, harder, with a drive that caused moisture to flood to the apex of her thighs. She would have crawled right up and onto him had he not broken the kiss.

His breathing was hard and ragged as he took a step back, as if composing himself. She could have sworn he mumbled something about having his wires crossed before he looked to her. "We should go now. They're gone."

"You heard them leave?" she asked.

"I heard them coming too."

Laney thought about what had happened in the coffee shop. How he'd vanished from the phone and an extreme sense of dread filled her, demanding she go outside—as if she had to get to someone in trouble.

Not someone, she thought. *Him.*

She took a step back. "Twilight Zone moment here."

"I can see where you'd think that. Can't be easy realizing shifters are real," he said.

She waved a hand in the air dismissively. "Not that part. That part I already knew. I was just waiting for proof to get everyone else to know too. Hello. What do you think I was trying to expose?"

He stared at her blankly.

She'd believed supernaturals were real for some time. Finding out she was on a date with one was something that took a moment to digest fully. "I was shocked *you* were one."

He didn't comment.

"Can I take a picture of you partially

shifted, or video-tape it for my blog post?" she asked, hope surging through her. The critics wouldn't be able to dismiss her if she had something concrete to show them. "It would really help if I had some proof to show everyone."

He remained stoic as he responded, "Humans aren't allowed to know about us."

"*I* know about you." She really didn't see the harm.

"I'm starting to think you don't count as most humans," he said flatly.

"Thanks." She eyed him more. She couldn't let this chance go to waste. "Would you be willing to let me interview you in secret about the supernatural so I can report on it? I wouldn't use your name."

"Did you miss the bit about humans can't know about us?" he asked.

"No. But hardly anyone believes my

theories anyway, so what would be the harm? And how many times in my life am I going to get a chance to interview a werewolf?"

"The answer is no."

"Is Bigfoot real?" she asked.

He nodded.

She smiled, excitement lighting up her eyes. "So he does sit in trees and think humans are stupid? Really?"

He groaned. "No. He's not real."

"But you said he was," she protested, her childhood hopes of one day catching the elusive beast gone.

"I like to get you going," Hagen returned, deadpan.

She put her hands on her hips and then walked in a slow circle, her mind spinning with everything that had happened from the moment she'd first heard his voice in the chatroom a week ago. She snapped around to face him. “Holy crapola, I trusted you from the word go. I gave you personal details about myself that I don’t tell anyone but my best friend. I agreed to meet you in person after only talking to you for a week online.”

He lowered his gaze. “I’m sorry, Laney. I couldn’t tell you the truth. I get that you hate me right now, but I need for you to listen to me. You need to come with me. It’s not safe for you to be on your own right now.”

She tipped her head to the side. “Hate you? What?”

“I thought that was what you were getting at,” he confessed.

“Hagen, I was about to tell you that something funky is going on because I don’t trust people easily and I certainly never sense danger around them.”

His eyes widened. “You sensed danger around me? When?”

"Phone call."

He took a really deep breath near her and she stepped back, her eyes wide. "Did you just sniff me?"

He blushed. "Yes."

"Eww. Do I stink?"

"Hell no!" he said loudly before clearing his throat. "Um, no. You do not stink."

"Why did you sniff me? Was it to catch my scent to track me later and murder me if I tell anyone about you?"

He gave her a droll look. "Yes. That is *exactly* why I smelled you."

She couldn't help but laugh at the look on his face. "Figured. I'm totally prey, aren't I?"

"Oh yeah. Totally."

She was about to joke more when the strangest urge to touch him again came over her. She did and then gasped as knowledge seemed to form in her gut. She looked to the end of the alley and then back to Hagen slowly. Without thought or a real understanding of what she was saying, she spoke, "He's closer than you think. Been searching for you. The one that got away. His personal toy. He's not done playing yet."

She swayed and Hagen wrapped his arms around her, steadying her, holding her tight. "Laney?"

Great, show him you're a nutjob. Harmony is going to love hearing that I flipped out and did the channel the freaky seer bit.

"I don't know why I said that. Sometimes that happens. I just speak and weird stuff falls out. I'm so sorry. You think I'm a total freak now, don't you?"

"I can turn into a wolf. Who am I to judge?" he asked, something off in his voice. "We need to go now."

"Are you taking me home?" she asked.

"Sweeting, they found you here at a coffee shop. Odds are, they know where you live."

She gasped. "My boys! They'll hurt my boys."

Hagen held her in place. "The veterans you take care of?"

She nodded. "I sort of jacked this old hotel and keep it running by hacking the city's grid and well, they all live there. They'll be hurt."

"Shit," said Hagen. "I need to get you somewhere safe and then I'll go to your place with my team and check on your boys."

"With your team?" she asked. As she thought more about it, she stepped back, realizing he was more than a werewolf. He was part of it all. "Craptastic! You're *The Man*. You're part of the establishment, aren't you?"

"The what?" he asked.

"One of the government's experiments. A super solider doing the establishment's bidding. How Big Brother makes us all obey."

He pursed his lips and she couldn't tell if he found her funny or annoying. "Your mind is a scary place. For one, I didn't start off as an experiment. I was born with the ability to shift into a wolf. Something unfortunate happened and then yes, I was experimented on, but no, it wasn't by *our* government."

She blew out a breath, a stray piece of her hair pushing back from her face. "Harmony was right. I can't believe she called it. I'm never going to live this down. Ever."

"Do I want to know what you're talking about?" he asked.

"Nope." She eyed him cautiously. How could she have missed all the key signs? He'd been so curious about her research, always asking about it, showing more interest than anyone ever had before. He'd even come out and confessed to having been in the military.

She'd never seen it coming. "I'm not a fan of the establishment."

"You don't say."

She couldn't help but smile. "I can't believe I agreed to a date with someone who works for *The Man*."

"To hell with the shifter bit," added Hagen with a grin.

"Ah, that's nothing," she said, lying. It was actually a huge freaking deal. Yes, she'd read about shifters existing and had been mining data for proof, but she'd never seen one face-to-face, let alone kissed one. She'd gone from zero to sixty in one evening, and heaven help her, she wanted to keep on going.

Ohmygod, I kissed a shifter.

She squeaked and stepped back from him. "We should go now. I need to see my boys."

"You and I will find a safe spot and then I'll call for backup. You'll wait somewhere safe and we'll see to your boys," he said forcefully.

"How are you going to do that? I saw your cell phone go flying into the street way back there by the coffee shop, and I dropped mine running to you."

This time, she was sure the way he looked at her said he thought "sweet, sweet, simple woman". Laney prepared to give him a huge piece of her mind but stopped as he turned his head, at first looking as though he heard something, but then seeming far away in thought.

Gasping, she realized what she was witnessing. Telepathic linking. She'd completely theorized it was possible for some supernaturals to connect via nothing more than their minds.

Holy shitake mushroom, I am a conspiracy theory goddess.

"You just mind-linked with your team,

didn't you?" demanded Laney.

Hagen gave her the placating expression again, and she considered grabbing one of the discarded pieces of trash on the side of the alley and throwing it at him. Making contact with the germs on it made her rethink her retaliation.

"Mind link?" he asked. "Never really thought of it that way, but yes. We mind link."

"Can you do it with anyone?" She put her hands on her head.

Was he doing it to her now?

Ohmygod, did he know how hot she thought he was?

She yelped.

Could he see her picturing him in nothing but his underwear? Her eyes widened.

Hagen took hold of her hands and lowered them from her head. "No. I can't read just anyone's mind. I can't even link with all supernaturals. I can do it with one of my pack members, either from the pack I was born to or the one I was brought into later in life, and I can do it with my teammates because we trained for years to be able to."

Was he telling the truth? It wasn't as though he'd been Mr. Honesty with her over the past week.

You kept things from him too.

She left her arms out, palms face up, ready to cover her head just to be sure. Where the hell was tin foil when she needed it? Maybe she could fashion one out of the bits and pieces of trash in the alley. She spotted some gun wrappers and tried to figure just how many she'd need to shield her entire head to keep him from being able to see all her deep, dark secrets.

Or at least keep him from reading how hot she thought he was.

She bent and lifted a candy bar wrapped. It looked as if it had been outside in the elements for some time. She held it up just before her forehead, her eyes narrowing on him.

He laughed. "I can't read your mind."

"I know. The foil is getting in the way. Interference."

"Actually," he said, touching her forehead and brushing something away. "I'm pretty sure it's not doing anything but letting those ants on it get on your head."

Ants?

Squeaking, she dropped the wrapper and then watched Hagen carefully.

Hagen caught her around the waist, snickering. "Laney, relax, please. I *promise* you that I can't read your mind."

"What did you tell your team members?" she asked, twisting in his arms.

"That they needed to split and that two

would need to get to the hotel to check on your boys," he responded. "I need the address."

With a heavy heart, she gave it to him. It felt like a betrayal to the men who trusted her so much. Even though her intentions were good, still she had just handed *the Man* a verbal map to where her boys were.

Hagen did his freaky look-off-into-nothing stare for a split second and then he took her hand in his. "We need to get to safety. Striker and Boomer are headed this way to rendezvous with us and make sure we can get you to a safe house."

"No. I want to go to the hotel. I need to check on my boys," she pressed.

Hagen's annoyance was hard to miss. "Laney, no. You're going to a safe house the minute my friends arrive."

Laney snorted. "That's what you think."

"People were just shooting at you. Can you

try to think about your own safety for five minutes?" he demanded.

She crossed her arms over her chest. He could get mad. She didn't care. She was more afraid of losing her family than of pissing off a werewolf. "The men who live in the building with me are like family to me. They *are* family. They're important to me. I don't want them hurt."

"You think I do?".

She shook her head. She didn't really believe he wanted them hurt either. "No."

"Then please, let's get somewhere safe. My team is coming. I promise they'll help."

"What if those people in the vans already went to my place?" she asked, knowing the answer. If the bad guys had tried her home, they would have found her boys and they wouldn't have stood a chance against them.

Hagen glanced away, confirming her

suspicions.

I could have cost my family their lives.

Laney picked then to lose it, the reality of her situation crashing over her. She considered flailing her arms about and screaming to anyone who would listen, but she realized it would do no good. The damage had probably already been done. If she'd allowed her quest for answers to outweigh her better judgment and gotten innocents caught in the crossfire, she'd never forgive herself.

There was no flailing. No screaming. Only immense sadness. The tears came fast as she sank against him. Suddenly, she felt very drained. More tired than she'd ever been in all her life. She suspected it was shock, but that didn't change how humiliated she felt.

Hagen didn't say a word. He lifted her as if she weighed nothing and walked with her down the alley in silence, letting her cry against his expensive shirt. Laney didn't protest being carried. She wasn't sure her legs would even work at the moment. She felt safe in his arms. Her connection to him seemed to grow with each step they took and Laney held tighter to him, never wanting him to let her go.

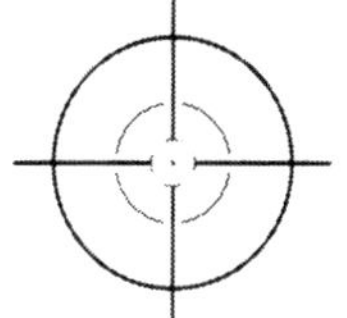

Chapter Ten

Bertrand listened as one of his men finished telling him the details of the other team he'd sent out after the girl. Hanging up the phone, he smiled. While the other team had failed to kill the woman in front of Hagen, they had caused Hagen's inborn need to protect his mate to kick in and Bertrand had little doubt that was who the female was to Hagen.

The Corporation had done a fair amount of digging on the girl, finding out she had roots in the Asia Project. That was a project close to his heart. It was one he'd learned of when he'd been recruited to join the Corporation and it was one he hoped to one day resurrect. It had been pure genius and so many successes had been birthed from it.

Sadly, they were scattered to the corners of the globe because those meddlesome Immortal Ops agents had stuck their nose where it didn't belong and then PSI had followed in after them, sniffing around even more facilities involved in the breeding programs. The do gooders had decided they knew what was best as far as scientific advancements, and had begun shutting down the facilities they'd been finding at an alarming rate.

The Corporation, in an attempt to salvage its research—the children—it had disbanded the breeding and incubation labs, hiding the children in foster homes, orphanages, anywhere they could, spreading them out, making it nearly impossible for anyone to track them.

Anyone but the Corporation, of course.

They had teams in place whose only duty had been to try to keep tabs on the subjects as they grew. Some the Corporation pulled in when they were in their teens or young adults, and continued their testing. Others, they simply observed. Laney was one of the watched. The Corporation had even had a hand in facilitating her adoption, putting her with trusted contributors. The girl had been somewhat of a problem child, getting too much attention for her hacking-related mischief. Twice a year when Laney was younger her adoptive parents would bring her to a doctor sanctioned by the Corporation so that he could run tests under the guise of a physical. The Corporation had all of her samples stored away.

The Corporation was smart, though, keeping those details out of any records, hiding them in codes that were nearly impossible to break just in case the records landed in the wrong hands, as had occurred after the fall of one of the facilities in France.

The young hacker had done the unthinkable. She'd actually hunted for them instead of the other way around.

Foolish girl.

She had virtually entered the lion's den and Bertrand was prepared to strike. He'd spent months sifting through samples on file from Asia Project females and even supernaturals yanked off the streets for testing, looking for ties and links, patterns.

He'd found one.

But Gisbert didn't want hear of it. Neither did the other scientists who all laughed at his theories that genetics were as big a factor in mating compatibility as destiny, which he put very little stock in.

Bertrand had wanted to find new ways to torture and torment Hagen, the man who had not given in and broken, so he'd looked at every avenue. When he began to experiment to see which samples on file caused a reaction in Hagen—a rise in blood pressure, an increase in aggression, a heightened state of arousal, he had thought that perhaps Gisbert was right—that there was no way to test for mates, but then Bertrand used Laney's samples. He knew he'd been correct. You could test for it.

Hagen had reacted and exceeded his expectations.

Bertrand knew she was the one who would light Hagen's fire. He had thought, though, that nature and this so-called destiny would have wanted a stronger female counterpart for such a headstrong male. Her hacking skills were impressive, but from what intel the Corporation had gathered on her, other gifts they'd hoped she'd develop because of the manipulations they'd done to her DNA in utero had not come to pass. She may be smart and good with computers but she was worthless other than that.

But not to Bertrand.

To him she was a way to break Hagen's spirit.

His prized soldiers had been sent to do what the regular ones had failed to. They would tear the hacker to pieces in front of Hagen and then they would bring Bertrand the man who could fix everything.

And then Gisbert and the others would finally see Bertrand for what he truly was. Not merely human. But rather, the man who was supposed to lead them in their revolution.

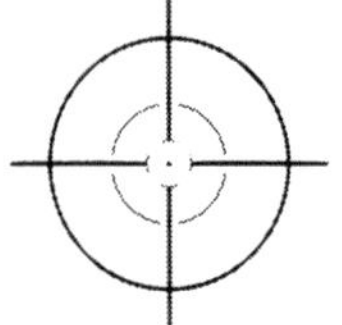

Chapter Eleven

James weaved in and out of the alleys and buildings, all while carrying Laney, until he was sure they couldn't be tracked with ease by anyone other than his teammates. The Pet Projects might be able to catch his scent, but he'd backtracked a good deal in hopes they wouldn't understand what was going on with his scent and trail.

The sounds and smells of the city streets were ones he was used to, having spent so much time on them over the past ten years, but it was different now that the Corporation—one man in particular, Dr. Bertrand—had altered James's genetic makeup.

There was no rhyme or reason as to why James's senses had gone over the top the moment he set eyes on Laney, when they'd been below standard for months. Hell, they'd been human-like. Was it a coincidence that he'd been about to meet her for the first time face-to-face when he lost control of himself? Duke had warned him. Had told him he was pretty much a ticking time bomb and that lack of sex wouldn't help.

Fucking Duke.

The asshole would love hearing he was right. He'd never let James live it down. Would probably nominate him for *Asshole of the Week* too. Then James would have his picture plastered on the hall wall next to the one of Boomer and Striker cutting a rug.

James took shallow breaths, hoping to stop the smells of the backend alleys. The sickeningly sweet stench of rotting garbage that had spent far too long in the sun burned James's nostrils and coated his throat. The wolf in him, who continued to stir, wanted him to shift fully and run from there, find woods, find nature, the concrete jungle not appealing to the animal in the least. And it wanted him to take Laney with him.

His wolf had good taste.

He tried to pull his senses back into himself. As Laney sniffled in his arms, he focused on *her* scent—a mix of vanilla and citrus. With extreme concentration he was able to isolate only her scent, blocking out the rest. Finally, he could take a deep breath. When he did, his cock decided it would hinder his ability to move quickly, hardening, wanting attention.

Not now.

Laney continued to weep against his chest, and he hated knowing that she was scared and upset over her friends. She was right, though—her boys were probably all dead. The Corporation had more than likely started with her home in their search for her. And the men she thought of as family wouldn't have been able to stand against the Corporation's highly trained mercenaries, especially if those mercenaries also included hybrids.

The Corporation would leave no witnesses to tell the tale of Laney's hacking. That was what the Corporation did—rid themselves of obstacles without hesitation.

With each step James took, the pain in his leg returned. His body, still not fully healed, protested his use of it, trying to convince him to stop, to sit, to rest. Unable to go forward anymore, he moved against a building and held Laney to him, refusing to set her down regardless what shape he was in.

He rested his head against the wall and closed his eyes, praying silently that Laney would come out of all this alive. He didn't want her life to be the price he paid for past sins. The price he paid for Christopher's death. He'd refused to listen to his visions then. Refused to see what they were trying to show him. He'd let his temper guide him rather than his gut and Christopher ended up dead. James would never be without the guilt of it. He'd never move fully past it.

How could he?

And now here he was, holding a woman who sparked his every interest, and all he could think was the Fates were going to take her to prove they could. To teach him a lesson.

Please. No. Me for her.

He squeezed her, unclear as to why he was willing to lay down everything for a woman he barely knew. His reactions to her began to play through his head—her scent, the fierce protectiveness, the constant and overwhelming need to claim her, the fact his dick didn't seem to have an off switch around her and the way he'd been drawn to her like he'd been drawn to no other.

Could it be his wires weren't crossed? Was she truly his mate? His destined woman?

He was a smart, highly educated man who had never understood why other males of his kind would talk of confusion when meeting their mates. How they could possibly misconstrue the signs spelled out before them. Now that he was suffering from the same affliction, James had to admit, it wasn't as clear-cut as he thought.

Did he trust his senses and his wolf, one that he had very little control of anymore and who been genetically altered, or did he trust his head? His head said the odds were astronomical that Laney would really be his mate—that by all evidence she was human or maybe even just slightly more than. Slightly more than still did not equal mating material. His body and his wolf said fuck statistics. They didn't give a shit what she was, only that she wear his mark on her.

My body and my wolf are going to get her killed.

She grunted, her hand tapping his chest. "Too tight."

"Sorry, sweeting." He desperately wanted to ravish her mouth once more but didn't dare attempt it. Not with the state she was in and what she was processing. As much as he wanted her, she had needs, and comfort was one of them now.

She looked up at him, her wide eyes red-rimmed from crying. "I didn't mean to bring this down on my boys. I never thought I'd get them hurt."

"I know," he said. "It's not in you to hurt them."

She cried more. "Gus wouldn't have understood what was happening. He doesn't talk. Casey and Bill look after him. They don't let him out of their sight. He wouldn't understand why men came to hurt him." She hiccupped as she sobbed. "And Gus lives every day thinking he's in 'Nam. The poor man. He survived those horrors only for me to get him killed because of my stupid curiosity."

"Shhh. Laney, don't do this to yourself," he said, adjusting his stance to try to take some weight off his bad leg.

"I did this," she said. "I was so stupid. I thought this would somehow answer my questions. That by following this trail it would lead me to answers about my birth and where I'm from, how I came to be. I didn't realize it would end like this."

James let her talk, knowing she needed to get it all out. Needed to talk it through in order to try to wrap her mind around it. None of what had happened could be easy for her to fully grasp. She was young and idealistic. She hadn't known the true horrors that existed in the world. The monsters hell-bent on destruction. She'd been curious and that was hardly a sin.

"Casey, he'd have put up a fight," she said softly. "He wouldn't take an attack lying down. Oh, Hagen, what have I done?"

"When my team gets here, we'll make sure the hotel is gone to," he said.

"So that the bodies of my family can be cleaned up before the public finds out, right?" she asked, venom dripping from her words.

"Laney, we don't know for sure that they are dead. We need all the facts before we go borrowing trouble and getting ahead of ourselves. They could be fine. We don't know anything yet."

She closed her eyes a moment. "Maybe, but I don't think so. I want to hope you're right but I don't know."

"I understand," he said and he did. He knew what carrying the guilt of getting someone you cared for killed could do to a person. And he was right, they didn't have anything concrete that said her boys were dead. Luck could have somehow found them, but he doubted it. He'd keep that to himself for now. She didn't need to hear it.

She leaned her head against his chest and

was quiet for a spell, caressing his chest. When she spoke, it was low. "Kiss me again."

"What?" he asked, sure he'd heard her wrong.

"Kiss me and make me forget. Even if just for a little bit," she pleaded.

Unable to deny her, James lifted her more and lowered his head. She came up in his arms, her hands going to the sides of his face as she attacked his mouth with hers. James nearly dropped her as fire shot right to his groin, centering there, hardening his cock at an alarming rate. The alpha side of him demanded he take the lead, that he prove he was in charge, but the other part of him, the one that was scared shitless of what Bertrand had done to him and that he might lose control let her set the pace in which they'd move forward.

Her tongue darted into his mouth and

James moaned, his hold on her tightening. He had to be mindful not to hurt her. He wanted this woman. Wanted to feel her body wrapped around his. Wanted to see her face when she came. Wanted to wake up with her still by his side come morning. It had been over a century since he'd felt anything close to raw need, and with a pang of remorse he realized what he'd felt for Elsbeth paled in comparison to what he felt for the woman in his arms—a woman, in truth, he barely knew.

Feels like I've known her forever and day.

His wolf pushed up fast and he swayed, fighting to stay upright, keep his beast down and hold Laney.

Claim her.

His gums burned, his teeth threatening to lengthen. He extended his fingers, fearing claws would emerge and in the process cut or harm Laney. That was completely unacceptable. James swallowed hard and nearly dropped Laney, just to put distance between himself and her. She didn't need to deal with him and his fucked-up alpha-male altered wiring. She had enough crap to deal with.

Her gaze swept up to meet his. She reached up, her lips parting as she touched just beneath his right eye. "Your eyes," she whispered. "They're not green anymore."

Oh shit.

James tensed, waiting for her to freak out about his shifted eye color. He hoped she'd remain calm since she'd taken the sight of his shifted arms without too much theatrics.

"They're… Hagen, they're red."

Red?

In shifted form his eyes were a light amber normally. Red? What the hell had the Corporation done to him? The horror of what he might do, what he might turn into—a single-minded killing machine—hit him with enough force to make him react. He staggered and Laney pushed to get down.

He let her, knowing she needed to be far from him.

The damn fool of a woman she grabbed for him, her fingers brushing over his skin, exciting him more. Was she crazy? Did she have a death wish?

"Hagen?"

He shook his head, leaping back from her. Missing her touch but wanting her safe. "No. I could hurt you."

With a dramatic huff, she rolled her eyes and approached him quickly. She slapped his arm lightly. "Knock it off. You just told me you wouldn't hurt me. Remember?"

He did remember and he'd been a damn fool to believe he was safe to be near. "That was before I realized I'm not in control of myself right now, Laney."

"Are you going to eat me?" she asked, turning one foot as she put a hand to her hip, standing in a cocky pose, eyeing him up and down. "You just made out with me. Was that how you tenderize your meat?"

"No. Well, shit. I don't think so," he said, looking at his hands which were still in human form. He held them out, staring at them, fearing at any minute they'd shift and he'd have no control over his wolf. That it might hurt Laney.

No!

His wolf thrust up at him, angry he'd even think such a thing. It wouldn't hurt her. Others, yes, but not her. Not the woman before him.

Laney groaned and reached for him, her hands going to his face. "Dude, seriously? You just saved my life. You put yourself over me to protect me from bullets and then carried me as I cried. If you were going to kill me, wouldn't you have just let the bad guys do it? I'd figure *the Man* would be all about bullet-saving."

"You accepted candy from strangers as a child, didn't you?" he asked, staring at her, realizing she must be crazy to trust him. He had frigging red eyes. He didn't even trust himself at the moment.

"Oh yes, buckets upon buckets of it," she replied with a sarcastic expression. "Are you done being stupid? You're not going to eat me."

His gaze eased down her, to the top of her short mini skirt. He wanted to slink it up and reveal her womanhood. Hell yeah, he'd eat her, just not in the way she was asking about.

Before he knew it, his hands were acting independent of his brain—roaming down her body, feeling her curves before settling on her hips. He yanked her to him and she gasped, looking up at him, her lips parting.

James kissed her and he didn't bother with being gentle either. He went strong and hard at her mouth, loving the taste of her. The little vixen pressed against him, pushing, almost scaling him—showing her eagerness and willingness to accept him.

His cock was more than pleased to have her on board with what it had been wanting to do for a week.

The more she rubbed on him, the more he realized he had about as much control over his orgasm in regards to Laney as he'd had when he was in his teens, and the very idea of a woman's body could make him spill his seed. The revelation wasn't one of his finer moments. He only hoped he didn't embarrass himself with her.

He sensed his wolf pushing at him,

wanting him to take their interaction past the point of acceptable. James didn't trust it or himself and he froze. He eased away from her slightly, remembering her words about if he would or would not eat her.

His gaze traveled back to her groin area. His mouth watered at the idea of being able to ease his tongue over her slit and taste her cream. Inhaling, he took in a deep breath, drawing in the scent of the very cream he wanted to sample.

She snapped her fingers. "Eyes up, Wolf Doc."

He looked up at her face and had to take a second to gather his wits. His brain was currently operating from between his thighs. Not in his head.

She gave him a knowing look. "Just because I'm a virgin doesn't mean I don't know what you were just thinking. I didn't even need that fancy mind-reading gig you've got going for you. Deduced that one all on my own."

He closed his eyes, ashamed at his behavior. He was acting like a randy rake. Hell, Striker behaved better. "I'm sorry."

"We can do that later," she said, a slight smile appearing on her face. That smile was so damn suggestive that James found it hard to see past it. "For now, I need to know what you know. What is really going on, and I need to know if my boys are all right."

Stunned, James stood there, his mouth agape. "Did you just tell me I could do what I think you said I could do later?"

She touched her lower lip and nodded. "Yep. I did."

He stiffened. "Let just anyone do that to you, do you?"

He couldn't stop the jealousy that rose

inside him.

"Don't be a douche," she snapped, bringing him back to his senses. "Of course not. Virgin, remember? Besides, you're not just anyone, are you, Hagen?"

He grimaced, embarrassed by the way he was acting. It was as if he'd suddenly taken dating tips from Striker or even Duke, prior to Duke's mating. Duke had been a complete ladies' man—never denied it, and the endless line of women he bedded knew the score. It was sex and that was all there was to it. Until Mercy. From everything James had heard, Mercy made him work for it.

Just like Laney is making you work for it. He cleared his throat, reminding himself that Mercy and Duke were mates. He and Laney were just…

What were they?

Friends?

Yes.

More than that?

Maybe.

But how much more?

He licked his lips. "No. I'm not just anyone."

"You're the man I've spent the last week forgoing sleep just to talk to. I told you a lot of things about myself. More than I told most."

"Laney, I was supposed to gather information on you," he said. He waited for her anger to come. He felt like the lowest of the lows. He'd used her to do his job. "You were supposed to be just a mission to me."

She sighed. "Hagen, I worked that out on my own when I saw the fur on your arms."

"Oh."

"Are you sure you're a doctor, because right now, I'm not believing it," she returned with a grin. "Seem a little slow on the response time and all."

James shrugged. "Most go-rounds I'm a healer of some sort. Once, I was a hot dog vendor."

"Most go-rounds? A hot dog vendor?" Her brows raised. "That is a story you are going to tell me more about, bucko. When we get through this, I want to hear all about that."

She wanted to see him again? Even after all he'd lied about? After being shot at? After he practically wolfed out in front of her?

"Are you crazy?" he asked.

"Certifiable," she answered. "How about you?"

"Pretty sure I have issues, yes."

She walked right up to him and touched his shoulder. He leaned, expecting to be slapped by her. She was well within her rights to haul off and let him have it. Instead, she kissed the tip of his nose. "Show me someone who doesn't."

He held her as he turned, hearing footsteps in the distance. He brought a finger to his lips, indicating the need for silence. She stood still and he turned his body, putting it before hers, shielding her as the footfalls grew louder. They were accompanied by something else. Wheels and rattling.

James prepared to attack whoever was coming around the corner. He put his hands out to his sides, ready to let the wolf up if need be. He'd do anything to protect her, even if it meant throwing caution to the wind and hoping for the best with a beast he wasn't sure he could control.

He waited with baited breath, wondering if it would be Bertrand who emerged. The sick fuck had eluded his team in France, managing to escape after juicing himself with his own concoctions for months—making himself some sort of supernatural blend. A hodgepodge with super-human strength and an already sadistic nature. James was different from many shifters in that he already had small amounts of Fae in him naturally. After what they'd pumped into him after they captured him, he had who knew what else swimming around in him.

James took a fighting stance, crouching despite the pain to his leg. The need to pace was great. He felt like a caged animal. He stood in place only because he didn't want Laney exposed to whatever evil was coming around the end of the building.

Get ready.

His heart hammered in his chest and his muscles tightened, expecting a battle.

An older man, wearing an old trench coat with patchwork spots dotting the elbows, came around the corner pushing a grocery cart. The cart was filled to the brim with trinkets, all reflecting the low lighting from the security lights at the end of the building. The man smelled human and as if he'd not had a bath in a while. Laney pushed on James's arms, forcing them down, as if she understood now that they were weapons in themselves.

"Emit!" she exclaimed, rushing around James to the homeless man. She stopped just shy of him. "What are you doing wandering around this time of night? You don't like the dark very much. Were the shelters full again?"

"Ms. Laney," he said, a smile finding his face. He was missing a few teeth, but the joy in his expression at the sight of Laney couldn't be denied. "Ms. Laney is okay. Casey was worried." The man twisted in a circle and pointed with one gloved hand at no one in particular. When he spoke, he threw his voice to be deeper. "No. Emit, it's not safe here tonight, Emit. You have to go to a shelter for the night. You can't be here. Bad things are afoot. Leave now, Emit. Go."

Laney gasped and touched the man's arm. "You went to the hotel tonight?"

Emit stopped spinning and nodded. "Casey said no. He made Emit leave. Said the bad was coming. Said Emit wasn't safe there."

Laney choked up. "Did you see Gus and Bill?"

"Gus has books. Bill has planes."

She pressed a smile that didn't look genuine to her face. "Go to Mary's on Second Street. Tell her I sent you. She'll find you a bed for the night. I don't want you trying to sleep on the streets."

"Ms. Laney is good people," he said, turning his cart in the other direction and heading off.

Laney returned to James's side. Touching her chin, she seemed to ponder what had just occurred.

"Emit isn't a fast walker," she said and inclined her head. "At his current pace, accounting for the number of times he stops and speaks with strangers and his affinity for picking up anything shiny, by my calculations, he would have been at the hotel before I even left to meet you for coffee. Before we even agreed to meet, Hagen. How would Casey know there was danger afoot *before* I even agreed to meet you for coffee?"

Surprised, James watched her, realizing she'd done the calculations that quickly. "Laney, did you just figure that all out in your head?"

She raised her shoulders, letting them fall again as if it were no big deal. It was a huge deal. He didn't like the feeling that was creeping up the back of his spine. Didn't like the idea that Laney could be more than met the eye. If she was, then the Corporation wouldn't rest until she was dead—or captured.

He would permit neither to occur.

If she's not human, she's mate material, he thought, need slamming through him once more for her.

He took her hand and began walking again, ignoring his leg as it protested all the activity. When they were far enough away from the fading sounds of sirens, he motioned to a crate, pushed up close to the backdoor of a building near them. "Rest."

"How will your people find us?" she asked.

He touched his nose. "Smell will lead the way."

She wrinkled her nose. "That is so weird."

"You get used to it."

His leg was now screaming in pain. He knew it must have showed on his face.

Laney lifted the crate and brought it closer to him. "You sit."

"I'm fine," he said sharply. He didn't like appearing weak in front of her. He'd once been fierce and now he felt like someone who needed a nursemaid.

"If you don't sit, I will run screaming through the alley and let the bad guys know where I am." From her stance, she looked serious.

He was about to call her bluff when he realized she was crazy enough to not be bluffing at all. With a grunt, he sat and gave her a hard look.

Damn purple-haired woman.

James glanced at her, loving the vivid streaks that matched her personality. There wasn't anything about her he didn't like.

"You can spank me later," she said with a sexy pout. "For now, rest your leg."

"I said I was fine," he replied, making a move to stand. He got a mental image of what it would be like to bend her over his knee, her sexy little backside offered up to him, and he paused, his hand going to his groin as he adjusted himself. "You had to bring up spanking, didn't you?"

She laughed and shrugged.

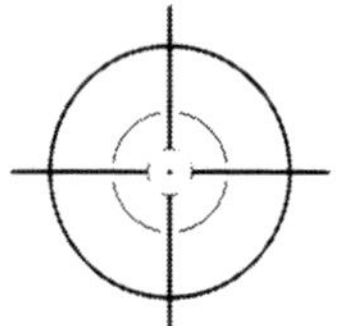

Chapter Twelve

Laney stared down at Hagen. He was a big man, muscular and tall with broad shoulders, yet something told her he was normally even bigger—more muscular. That he wasn't quite himself. He was hurting and she couldn't stand to see him in pain.

She put her hands on his shoulders and held him down. "I get that I'm not very strong compared to you, but if you try to get up, I will body-slam you."

He glanced at her arms. "Actually, I was going to comment on just how strong you are."

She laughed. "Casey tells me all the time to mind my strength. Like I'm some sort of Amazon warrior princess."

"You spend a lot of time with this Casey," he said, his voice off.

"We've been over this. He's like family to me." She glanced around and spotted a door. She left Hagen long enough to check it out. It was locked with only with an old rusty chain and a padlock. She nearly laughed. Like that would keep someone out.

Reaching into the back of her hair, just under her ponytail, Laney felt for her bobby pin. She'd had a strict never-leave-home-without-one policy since she was twelve. They came in handy and often helped to get in or out of things.

In this case, in.

She pushed it into the padlock's keyhole and did what she'd taught herself to do years ago—she picked the lock. It popped open and she turned to tell Hagen to follow her, only to find him standing directly behind her, watching her with amused eyes.

"I'm on a date with a criminal, aren't I?" he asked, his eyes crinkling with mirth.

"Could be worse." She clucked her tongue. "You could be on a date with a werewolf."

"Fair point."

"Come on," she said, looking back at him, enjoying the feel of doing something that fell into shades of gray according to right or wrong. "Let's go in and get off the streets for a little bit. Will your team find us if we're not out in the open?"

"Yes." He followed her in, his large body

crowding her decidedly smaller one. Heat moved through her and Laney was sure the building must be on fire because all that heat couldn't be coming from her, could it?

She moved slowly in the darkened corridor before Hagen put a hand on the small of her back, causing additional heat to rush over her. He eased around her, his hand finding hers as he took the lead.

"I can see in very low lighting," he said, the timbre of his voice licking at her insides, making them feel as if butterflies filled her. Harmony would laugh at her, calling her naïve in the ways of men.

Laney gripped his hand and she followed close at his heels. She wasn't sure what he meant by low lighting, because it seemed pretty much pitch black to her until Hagen pushed open a door and light spilled out. Several old, beat-up washing machines and dryers lined the walls. Each was coin-operated.

Hagen turned and lifted her, his large hands fitting nearly all the way around her waist. She gasped as he pulled her close and then set her upon a washer. He stood there, his body pressing to hers.

She couldn't stop herself from touching his face. What was it about him that drove her so nuts with lust? Her girly bits wanted his manly bits in bad way. To the point they were about to beg. And her girly bits had never begged for anything in her twenty-two years.

This man could punch my V-card any day.

"You should sit," she said, needing to say something to fill the silence between them. Having him sit and rest his leg seemed much more safe for her V-card than what she'd wanted to say, which had been *do me*.

Harmony would have loved that.

"Hagen," she said, a thought hitting her. "I

need to check in with my friend. I need to make sure she knows to stay away from my place."

"If the Corporation is as good as you, what do you think they'll be doing?" he asked.

She pondered his question and then felt deflated. "Monitoring my known associates."

"They'll know if you reach out, Laney," he said. "They'll know and it could get your friend hurt."

"Harmony lives a pampered, rather sheltered life," she pushed. "I don't want her brought into this. I dug my own grave."

"You're not dead yet." He winked.

But she'd probably gotten her boys killed.

Casting her gaze downward, she felt the tears wanting to return again. Felt the severity of the situation soaking through her every pore, settling around her neck like a noose. "I shouldn't have wanted to find out about my birth and its weird circumstances. I should have left well enough alone. I shouldn't have let my curiosity get to me when Blue Butterfly gave me the tip on the Asia Project. It's been nothing but a curse."

Hagen put his hands on her bare thighs. "What did you say?"

She sniffled. "My stupid hunt for who I am and where I come from got me here."

"Did you say Asia Project?" he asked.

She nodded.

"What do you know of it?" he asked.

Laney did her best to keep herself together. Breaking down more wouldn't fix anything. Nothing would. "It's linked to my birth. I was part of it somehow. My biological mother was in it while she was pregnant with me."

Hagen stepped back and spun, punching the cinderblock wall of the building's laundry room. The room shook and Laney half expected the place to crumble around them. She yelped.

Hagen kept his back to her, and when she saw the fur on his arms, she knew why—he was doing that wolf thing again. She knew she should have been terrified of him, but she wasn't. He felt safe to her. Didn't matter how furry he got.

"What is it?" she asked. "Do you know more about it?"

"I do, but you shouldn't know the details. You'd be in even more danger," he answered, his back still to her, his voice deep.

"More than people already wanting me dead? How much more dead could I get?" she asked with a snort.

When he faced her, his green eyes were red again and his shoulders and neck seemed bigger than before. "They'd stop wanting to kill you and start wanting to capture you. And trust me," he said, lowering his head, his words slurring a bit as if he was having trouble speaking clearly. "You do not want to be captured."

Her gaze went to his leg. Was that what had happened to him? Had he been held prisoner by these madmen? Rage trickled over her and she sat up straight, her feet dangling.

"Tell me who hurt you," she insisted.

Hagen's jaw worked back and forth. It was then she realized his wolf thing was impeding with his speech. Her anger faded fast, replaced with concern for him. She put a hand out, waiting, knowing he'd come to her. He did. She touched his furry arm. "My date with a werewolf has been something indeed."

Laney watched as the hair on his arms receded, disappearing as if it was never there. She let out a low whistle. "Coolest thing ever! If I throw a ball, will your instincts tell you to chase it?"

Hagen's neck and shoulders returned to regular, but still large, size and a slow smile crept over his handsome face. "No. But don't throw a stick or I won't be able to help myself."

Her eyes widened. Was he serious? "Really?"

He laughed. "No."

She pushed lightly on him. "Jerk."

He caught her hand and kissed the back of it. "Laney, tell me more about yourself. Tell me what you don't tell anyone."

"I'm good with computers and anything tech related," she said.

He gave her an even look. "That I know. Tell me something I don't."

"Hagen, I'm not just good. I'm freakishly good. Like, I can work them and do things with them others can't. Sometimes, I'm faster than the computer at processing the information I'm taking in."

He nodded and she kept going.

"And Casey tells me I'm strong. Stronger than I should be for a girl, I guess."

"Not for a girl," answered Hagen. "For a human."

"Oh." She thought more on it all. "And at times I just get strange vibes from people and then I sometimes say things that don't make a ton of sense to me. Harmony jokes that I have a sixth sense."

"She might not be wrong." he said. "Anything else?"

She shook her head. "No. That is it. Am I a freak? From what I could uncover about my birth mother, she was experimented on when she was pregnant with me. I couldn't find out much beyond that—well, and that she was part of some Asia Project. I haven't been able to find out more on it. I was digging for information and that was when I came across some files that suggested the government had knowledge about supernaturals but was hiding it from the public."

"And let me guess, that led you straight to the Corporation," he said.

She nodded. "Sort of. I had a little help with being pointed at them. They'd been on my radar for nearly a year, and then two weeks ago one of their facilities in France had a series of explosions. Their cover story didn't add up."

"No. It didn't. I was there. It wasn't pretty," he said.

She looked to his leg. "My gut is telling me you were hurt and it has something to do with them."

He huffed. "Your gut is not wrong. But I don't want to talk about my time being held there."

She flinched. He'd been held there? She'd

read what they did to their captives. As she touched Hagen more, a sinking feeling came over her. "Test Subject 87P?"

The veins in his thick neck worked and tension rolled off him. "Yes."

She cupped her mouth. "Oh, Hagen."

He lifted his head, the red gone from his eyes. "I don't want you to pity me."

"Pity you?"

Was the guy for real?

"What they did was horrible. They're monsters. All I want to do is wrap my entire body around you and hold you, just to show you what love is."

Love?

Why had she brought that up?

She didn't throw the L word around with reckless abandon. She kept it closely guarded, as she'd never trusted anyone enough to set it free.

While she was lost in thought, Hagen touched her lower lip with his thumb. The action was oddly erotic and she couldn't help but ease a little closer to the edge of the washing machine in order to close the gap between them.

He bent his head and moved his thumb, his lips pressing to hers. The kiss was chaste, unlike their others, but it still packed a wallop.

"Thank you," he said.

She took hold of his shirt, keeping him close. He cupped her face, his lips returning to hers. This time, the kiss was anything but PG-rated. Laney's legs wrapped around his waist as if they had a mind of their own. Apparently, they were in league with her girly bits and on a mission to get her V-card punched.

His kiss increased and Laney found herself untucking his shirt and pulling it up, her fingers finding his undershirt. There was simply too much material between the two of them. With a groan, she pulled up hard on his undershirt, their lips still together, their tongues darting and weaving from one another's mouths.

The minute Laney's fingertips brushed over Hagen's hot, hard abdomen, her hormones rocked into outer space. She sucked on his lower lip, and then Hagen's hands were suddenly seemed to be everywhere at once and she loved it.

Loved him touching her.

He tugged lightly on her black, fitted top, lifting it at a snail's pace, as if giving her ample time to change her mind. She broke the kiss and took his hands in hers, lifting them and placing his hands under her shirt on her bare skin.

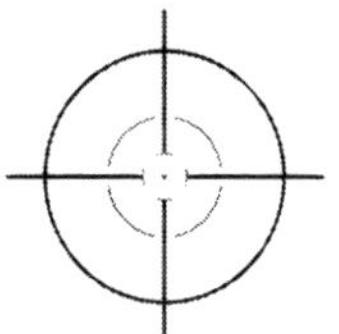

Chapter Thirteen

James traced circles over Laney's sides, her skin feeling soft and smooth under his fingers. It took all his control to continue to restrain himself. He wanted to lift her off the washer, wrap her legs around his waist and drive home, ramming his cock deep inside her. His fingers made their way into her hair and he tugged lightly on her ponytail, forcing her head back more, wanting to devour her.

Slow down.

His body didn't want to slow down or listen to his head. He inched her shirt up more, his fingers skimming the undersides of her bra. Need took hold of him and he fought to think clearly. He needed her. Nothing else mattered. He wanted to feel her body from the inside. He wanted to taste her flesh, sink his shifted teeth into her neck and bite while he pumped in and out of her.

Claim her!

His inner beast shouted at him and James's mind was such a mess of emotions and sexual lust that he couldn't fully grasp why his wolf was yelling such a thing at him.

If you do this and can't control yourself, you could kill her.

That did it. That cooled his sexual appetite. With slow, stiff movements, James jerked away from her. Her taste on his lips and the remembered feel of her torso and being so close to touching her breasts was burned into his brain.

Laney stared up at him, bewilderment upon her face. "Hagen?"

He opened his mouth to comment but stopped when every built-in alarm he had began to go off, firing incoming details at him with a frenzy. Something was wrong. Something was close.

More than one something.

The hybrids!

With one arm, James grabbed Laney from the top of the washer and spun with her, just as the laundry room door was kicked inward, sending pieces of the wood splintering in all directions—including into James's upper back. Ignoring the pain, he kept moving with her, putting her in the opposite corner before setting her on her feet and spinning fast, his claws coming out with lightning-fast speed. He knew what he must look to Laney with his upper body partially shifted. He couldn't worry about that now. He needed to handle what had sought them out.

A vampire-wolf hybrid.

He wasn't sure if it had started out life as either of the two, but whatever the Corporation had done had left them a mix of both, and they were nasty cusses.

The creature stood there, in even less human form than James, snarling, spittle running down its chin. It stared wild-eyed past him at Laney and James knew then that it had her scent, that it was tracking her and couldn't give a shit about him.

Well, it had another think coming.

"What the ever-loving-crack-smoking-butt-ugly kind of creature is that?" asked Laney, her voice high, her fear riding the air.

My woman has a gift for words.

He stayed facing the hybrid, smart enough to avoid taking his eyes off it. James soaked in the way it moved, his own wolf reading the other, sizing him up. When the hybrid lunged for Laney, James was already there, reacting, impeding its ability to get her. He slammed the hybrid backwards into a clothes dryer. The sound of metal crunching under the weight of the supernatural was near deafening.

James didn't pause or let up in his counter-assault. He grabbed for the hybrid, remembering all too well what it had been like to be ambushed by similar ones and then subjected to tortures by them as they did their masters' bidding.

The temper he'd fought so long and hard to learn to control surged to the surface. It took the lead.

Not the wolf.

Not James.

Just pure hatred.

His vision blurred for a moment, filling with red before everything became clear—crystal clear. Ripping the man up, James snarled as he twisted his hand, snapping the man's neck with ease. He sensed another hybrid coming and used the body of the first as a weapon, turning and then launching the weight of the limp man at the newcomer.

The broken neck may or may not have killed the first hybrid. Being immortal meant one could bounce back from a lot, and he'd seen several hybrids return from what would have killed a normal supernatural. James wasn't sure if this one would heal his injuries rapidly and rise again, but with the amount of adrenaline and rage consuming James, he didn't care. He would annihilate them all. It didn't matter how many times they came back for more.

The second hybrid pushed to his feet, his fangs flashing and claws swiping at the air. James moved with such speed that it felt as if his opponent had started to move in slow motion. The doctor side of him knew why it was happening—the Corporation had amped him up, making him more of everything he'd already been. He doubted very much that they ever thought those very traits would be turned against them. They were arrogant enough to believe themselves untouchable. Feeling as if he had all the time in the world, James reached up and snatched hold of the hybrid's wrist. He yanked hard.

Very hard.

Too hard.

James struggled to come out of the red haze as he realized he held an arm in his hand but no body was attached to it. The anger, the rage, the hate kept control and James twisted, his gaze landing on Laney.

I'm a fucking monster.

Shock coated her face. She had the back of her hand to her mouth, her skin even paler than normal as she stared at the arm he was holding.

James managed to get enough common sense through his wolf and his rage that he dropped the arm. It landed with a splat in a puddle of blood that was pooling and spreading in Laney's direction.

James reached for her and she screamed, pressing herself against a washing machine. "You ripped his limb off."

He grimaced. There was nothing he could say. Yes, he'd done it. Yes, she'd witnessed the entire act. All he could do now was get her to safety. The hybrids traveled in groups, and these two wouldn't be alone.

"Laney."

"Holy crapola," she whispered, her attention on the floor as she practically crawled onto the washer to keep the blood from getting all over her. "You just pulled it off like it was a wing on a fly."

James clenched his fists, his claws digging into the palms of his hands, reminding him of their differences. He was an animal. She was not.

She opened her mouth, but no sound came out, her gaze wild and focused beyond him. On the door.

Behind you!

James tipped his head, feeling as if she'd screamed directly into it. How had Laney done that? How had she projected her voice into his mind?

He didn't have time to figure it all out.

Something massive slammed into him from behind. James threw his arms out, breaking its hold, and then spun, charging the mostly shifted hybrid. Going low, James put his shoulder into it, ramming directly into the hybrid's midriff, knocking him backwards. With the momentum James was carrying, he went too, right out the laundry room door and into the hallway where he was yanked to the right by yet another hybrid.

They were everywhere.

James ducked and came up, striking one in the nose, sending bone fragments into the hybrid's brain. It fell backwards into the wall and the other behind it tripped, falling at James in a way that James simply grabbed its head and snapped its neck as well.

He turned, claws erect, and took out the throat of another. He was about to bite the shoulder of one more when Laney's screams rent the air, pulling his attention in her direction and off the men trying to kill him to get to her. The red around James's gaze thickened as he saw Laney being carried out of the building by a hybrid.

His woman kicked and thrashed to no avail. James shut off and it was he who reached for the wolf instead of the other way around.

Come. Be free. Protect her!

The wolf obeyed and James surrendered himself to it, understanding there was a chance he'd never gain control or shift back to human again. She was worth the risk.

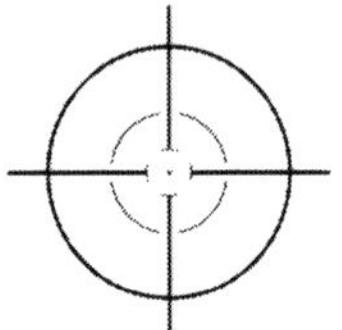

Chapter Fourteen

Laney dug her fingernails into whatever the hell the thing was that was carrying her like a sack of potatoes. She bounced around, nausea rising. The thing holding her was built like a tank. A hairy, smelly tank with pasty grayish-blue skin showing through its patches of fur. She slapped at it more, wiggling, twisting, and finally gaining some room to move. She turned as much as she could and went for the eyes, like Casey had taught her to do when all else failed.

She scored a direct hit. Her thumbs poked into the creature's eyes and Laney had to fight to keep from being sick as there were two rather loud popping sounds right before the creature dropped her and grabbed its face, blood running down its cheeks.

Laney hit the ground hard, her side taking the brunt of the fall, and it knocked the wind out of her for a moment. When she got her bearings, she turned to see more of those things pouring out of the building she'd just been in. The building Hagen was *still* in.

"Hagen!" she screamed, pushing to her feet, planning to charge in and do whatever she could in an attempt to save the day. Something caught her by the arm and she turned fast, delivering a wicked kick to the man's kilt-covered groin.

"Och!" the man yelled, bending forward, releasing her arm.

Kilt-covered?

Why the hell was a bad guy in a kilt?

She looked again. And why was he wearing a black t-shirt that said *Have Stake Will Use It*? Over it he had on a gun holster, the shoulder kind, and two pretty big weapons. It took her a minute to pull her gaze from the guns as she wondered why he hadn't just shot her. The others had tried.

Stop waiting around for it.

This certainly was not how she imagined paranormals to be when she'd been on her quest to unlock the truth of them. Whatever he had on, he wasn't going to touch her. She made a move to kick him again when a different man leapt in front of the one in the kilt and put his arms up. The newcomer's black shirt said *Got*

Sparkle. And this guy looked completely different from the kilt-wearing redhead with the thick beard. He also had multiple weapons covering his body.

"Whoa, we come in peace there, little punk rock girl," he said, hands still out like that was going to somehow make him magikally less threatening. Not after what she'd seen since finally coming out of her computer cave.

I'm never leaving my hacking haven again.

Ever.

She eyed the man who was decked out in black leather and enough piercings to possibly make a silver vase should he ever have them melted down and repurposed. His hair looked almost blue-black in the dim glow from the security lighting of the other building. He had enough eyeliner on to make Laney and her normal heavy-makeup-wearing ways seem bland. His violet gaze held no malice. His features were strange, yet oddly stunning. What's more, they were familiar, but she couldn't put her finger on them. When it hit her, she pursed her lips. Feline. He somehow managed to remind her of a cat.

"Seriously? You, of all the people here, are calling me punk?" asked Laney.

The man shrugged. "Got your attention off trying to kill Striker."

Striker?

She'd heard Hagen mention the name. She kept her attention on Violet-Eyes. "Are you Boomer?"

"I am," he said. "Where is James?"

Laney turned to point at the building's back entrance and found it bursting open. One of the foul-smelling, nasty creatures that had grabbed her was there, on its back in the alley, sliding to a stop while the biggest friggin' wolf she'd ever seen rode the thing's body like a surfboard.

She blinked, sure she'd lost her mind.

Nope. There was still a huge wolf on a stinky monster.

Never, ever, ever leaving my computer cave again.

Boomer pulled Laney back more and then gasped. "What the fuck?"

Striker, who was still nursing his groin, looked up, his eyes widening. "Do my eyes deceive me or is that James?"

"On spinach!" yelled Boomer. "His wolf is huge. What the hell did they do to him?"

"Gave him a hell of a vitamin regimen, apparently," the Scot said.

Laney said nothing as the wolf they were claiming was Hagen, though she had no actual proof since she'd never seen the guy fully shift into anything yet, bit down, removing the creature's neck.

"Eww," she said, wrinkling up her face at the sight of it all. Strangely enough, she was less freaked out by the fact he'd killed the creature than by the knowledge that nasty creature's flesh and blood were in Hagen's mouth. A mouth she'd only just been kissing moments before. A mouth she thought she wanted to kiss again, but not with creature bits in it.

"Aye, lass, eww," said Striker, his Scottish brogue thick. He rubbed his groin in an unabashed way, shaking his head. "You had to kick me there? Of all places, there?"

She got the feeling most of his deductive reasoning occurred between his legs, so she'd more than likely impeded his thought processes. He kept rubbing himself, as if he didn't care who saw him do what, and she wondered if he'd say to hell with it and lift his kilt to check his man parts out.

Seemed the type.

"You've a hell of a kick, Punky," he said.

Punky?

She eyed his groin, considering kicking him in it again. Friend of Hagen's or not, she'd do it.

"Easy, tiger." He stepped back, cupping himself before nodding to Boomer. "Eleven o'clock."

Boomer twisted, thrust Laney at Striker and then punched out at a bad guy. This one looked mostly human except for the eyes. They were red, like Hagen's currently were—again. Boomer bent, his movements very catlike as he came up, fur sprouting on his forearms as he sprang up at the bad guy, hitting him head-on in midair. The collision was so epic that it seemed to shake the ground they were all standing on.

It's like Clash of the Furry Gods.

Another one of the ugly creatures descended from above and she did a double take.

Holy-crap-on-a-pita-chip, it has wings!

It didn't matter how much training Casey had given her, there was no way she was prepared to take on a flying, pasty, smelly monster. In place of yelling, which she didn't think she'd be judged upon at a later date because the damn thing had wings, Laney had a burning desire to have a cell phone handy to record the creature for her post on what walked among humans.

Or in this case, flew.

Her loyal blog readers would think this was the coolest thing ever.

Striker leapt up and over Laney as if she wasn't even there, landing before her, pushing the winged-creature away. She had to admit, she was somewhat impressed with the Scottish guy. He'd done that jump without taking a running start or anything.

The winged thing hissed at him and he shook his head. "When you signed up for testing and to be an evil minion, did you know it was goin' to leave you lookin' like that? If so, yer a dumbass. If you did nae know, all I can say is fine print is apparently verra important. The devil is in the details."

The creature charged Striker and Striker moved an arm out gently, pushing Laney to a new spot just behind him as the two of them stepped out of the way of the attack. The creature went right past them and head first into the brick wall.

Another bad guy came out of nowhere and struck Striker from the side, knocking him in the direction of the wall too. There was a struggle and then a huge bang as the creature lurched back from Striker.

The Scot sat on the ground, his kilt fanned out in a way that only barely kept his private parts covered, gun in hand, grinning.

The guy was grinning.

Lunatic.

He looked past her. "Lass, get down!"

She did. He may have been crazy but he was on her side—at least she hoped. He fired again and the sound echoed off the buildings, making it hard for her to hear for a few seconds that managed to feel more like minutes. Turning, Laney saw Boomer's mouth moving but couldn't make out what he was saying.

Danger!

The word felt as if it were thrust into her mind. It wasn't her own thought though. She knew that. Oddly, she thought of Gus, as if he had anything to do with what was happening. Wherever the thought came from, something deep down told her to listen.

Gasping, she spun, acting on instinct and years of self-defense training from Casey. She came around in time to reach as one of the creatures extended a clawed hand at her throat. Laney threw up an arm, deflecting the blow as she punched the thing in the gut with more force than she thought she had in her. She hit it so hard it went hurtling backwards, in the direction of Hagen, who was still in wolf form. He leapt upon its back, making short work of it.

Boomer grabbed her, yanking her back and out of harm's way. He turned her and began looking her over. "Are you hurt?"

She rubbed her ears. "How can you hear anything?"

Striker was suddenly next to her as well. "Lass, are you harmed?"

She shook her head.

The two men glanced at the creature she'd fought with and then back to her. They both boldly sniffed the air. She groaned. "Really?"

"I smell Fae," said Striker.

Boomer flashed a wide smile. "I smell panther."

Hagen made a strange growling noise that sounded muffed. When she looked at him, she nearly lost control and threw up. He had a huge piece of creature meat hanging from his mouth, as his red eyes found her.

Laney groaned and looked to Striker who had his nose wrinkled as well. "Lass, he normally has much better eatin' habits. He's into healthy livin'."

"Does that include eating gargoyles?" she asked, fascinated with what she was seeing, yet completely repulsed as well.

Striker eyed the now dead slab of creature. "I do nae think it's a gargoyle. More of a bat thingamabob." He turned to Boomer. "Hey, *Batman*, something to look forward to."

"Suck me, Milkshake." Boomer moved alongside them and also made a face, indicating he thought seeing Hagen's wolf eat the creature was disgusting too. "Striker, pull James off the…what the hell is that?"

"I vote gargoyle," said Laney, lifting a hand in the air, feeling oddly at ease with all she'd witnessed so far. "Redhead here votes part bat."

"Well, it's all ugly," added Boomer.

She and Striker nodded.

Laney found herself bonding with the two men under the strangest of circumstances. Striker looked to Boomer and put out his hand. "Before I stop James, give me yer phone."

"Why?" asked Boomer.

"I want a picture of this to show James later when he's lecturin' me on eatin' less red meat."

Laney laughed and found she couldn't seem to stop laughing. She knew it was a mix of shock and adrenaline, but that didn't matter. The giggle-fit kept going.

Striker eyed her. "Should you nae be passed out or screamin'?"

She lifted her hands to suggest she was clueless. "Is that how one should respond to this?"

"'Tis how girls do," he said snidely.

She looked at his groin again.

He pursed his lips. "Did I say girls? I meant to say…well, I do nae know. Stop lookin' at my most prized possession like you wish him harm."

She laughed more.

He lifted a brow. "By chance are you part pixie too? They've a thing for laughing under stress, and apparently, if you are, they're procreating at an alarming rate."

"I'm a hacktivist," she said proudly.

He nodded and then stopped, mid-nod, eyeing her. "I've no idea what that is."

She smiled and giggled more.

He made a move to go for Hagen and Hagen turned, his red eyes ablaze, his long teeth showing as he snarled and then snapped at Striker's hand. Striker yanked his arm back.

"Bad wolf," he said sternly.

Hagen growled and went low as if ready to attack.

Striker made a move for Laney. "Lass, you do nae want to be too close to him. He's nae safe to be near right now."

Hagen was suddenly between them, taking a bite at Striker. He missed. Just barely.

Gasping, Laney swatted the massive wolf. "Hagen, no!"

She froze.

So did Striker.

Had she just corrected an enraged werewolf?

She replayed the events in her head.

Oh crap.

"Lass," said Striker, drawing Hagen's attention to him. "Back up verra slowly and get behind Boomer." He stared past her. "You kept a vial of that sedative Mercy gave us?" he asked Boomer.

"No. Corbin frisked me right after he did you," answered Boomer. "Said we weren't allowed to use it to get high. He's a killjoy."

"Aye, the Bloody-English-Bastard-Out-to-Steal-My-Country wouldnae know a good time if it bit him in the arse."

Laney put her hands on her hips. Her saviors were talking about getting high? "Focus on Hagen. And not illegal substances."

"Och, it's nae illegal. *Yet.* Besides, I do nae

need to focus on James. He's focused enough on me, lass," said Striker, staying very still. "Cannae be sure but I think he has plans to try to eat me too."

"It's probably your milkshake magnetism," added Boomer dryly from beside her.

Lost, Laney glanced between them. "Serious moment here, boys."

"Nah," said Boomer. "We've been in worse situations, and it's not the first time a teammate has tried to eat us. Just over a week ago our teammate Duke took a chunk out of each of us when he was stuck in wolf form."

Yelping, she turned to face Boomer, her face ashen. "A shifter can get stuck in shifted form?"

He swallowed hard, looking as if he didn't want to tell her the answer. "Um…yes?"

That meant Hagen could get stuck in wolf form. She shoved at him, but didn't budge him. "Fix him!"

"It's not that easy," he returned. Boomer reached for her and Hagen rushed past her, snapping at Boomer.

Full up on crazy and hard to wrap her mind around scenarios, Laney reacted, swatting Hagen hard on the top of the head. "Enough!"

He stopped and sat as if he wasn't just about to eat his friend and hadn't been snacking on the stuff of nightmares only moments prior.

She watched Hagen, waiting for him to change back into himself. He didn't. "Change. Stop being all wolfy."

Still nothing.

"Lass, he cannae understand you right now," said Striker. "He's in a deep shift. The kind that leaves the man lost and the wolf in charge. We worried this would happen to him with all he's been through."

Boomer took a large breath in and his violet gaze widened. He stared between the big wolf and Laney. Then his attention went to Striker. "Do you smell that?"

Laney lifted her arms, and gave up trying to look ladylike as she sniffed her armpits. Why did they all keep smelling her?

Striker inhaled and then paused. A second later, he whistled. "Two in a month. What are the odds?"

"Two what?" she asked.

Boomer looked to Hagen and ignored her question. "Doc, if you're in there, anywhere, she's safe. We're not the enemy. We'd never hurt your mate."

Mate?

Laney was so lost.

What was he talking about?

Striker nodded. "Aye, James, we'll nae

harm her. We'll protect her as we would you."

"Your woman is safe," said Boomer.

Laney stiffened. "His woman? What? I'm not his woman. We just officially met tonight."

Striker laughed as he stepped over the carcass of the winged thing, keeping his eye on Hagen the entire time. She didn't blame him. Hagen had already eaten how many things?

"Lass, you most certainly are his woman. See how he guards you? Do you notice he only comes at us when we make a move to touch you?"

She thought more on it.

Striker was right. Hagen had only gone at him and Boomer when they'd tried to make contact with her.

Huffing, Laney looked at Hagen. "You lied to me. You took me on a date that is seriously the worst date in the history of ever. You ate not one, not two, but at least three of those nasty butt-ugly things, and now you're trapped in wolf form? LabLupus, if you don't change back right this second, I swear to you that I'm never going to speak to you again. Worse than all that, you work for *The Man*!" She stomped her foot. "Your woman, my ass, bucko."

Boomer snorted. "Yeah, that will work."

No sooner had the words left his lips than Hagen began to change shape. If she'd blinked, she'd have missed it. He was suddenly there, standing before her, wearing nothing but what he'd been born in.

Her cheeks flushed as her gaze raced to his groin. It was as if her eyes didn't really care that her brain knew better than to look. They were stealing a peek come hell or high water. And, oh boy, there was a lot to peek at.

If that punched my V-card, I might not be able to walk for weeks.

Hagen attempted to shield his nudity with his hands. It didn't work. With a sheepish grin, he looked at her. "I know our coffee date has been less than perfect, but the odds of me getting to take you out to dinner at some point are…?"

"I just watched you eat a bat thing," she said. "I'm not sure I'll ever be hungry again."

Hagen sighed.

A shaky smile reached her lips. "But I'd be willing to give it a try."

Joy filled his green gaze and she had to fight to stay in one place and not run to him and throw her arms around his neck. She wanted to make contact with him and soon.

What is it with you? You're not one of those girls.

She stared harder at Hagen and realized he was her man.

Oh crap. That means I am his girl.

She licked her lower lip and held out her hand before realizing if he took her hand, his man bits would show. Hagen seemed to realize it too. He glanced at Boomer and let out a long breath. "I don't suppose you have extra clothes in your car?"

"Come on, Doc," said Boomer. "Let's get you dressed and a cleanup team called in."

"What about my boys?" Laney asked. She needed to know what had happened to them.

Hagen glanced at his friends. "Have either of you had any contact from Duke or Corbin since they splintered off to go to the hotel?"

"No," said Striker.

Boomer shook his head.

Laney's heart sank.

Striker pulled off his t-shirt and handed it to Hagen. "Here. Will do us no good parading you around the city naked."

Hagen's lips drew to one side as he held

the shirt in front of his groin. "Thanks."

"You've worn worse," added Striker. "Captain should have checked in by now."

"Something is off," said Boomer.

Laney nodded. Something was really off.

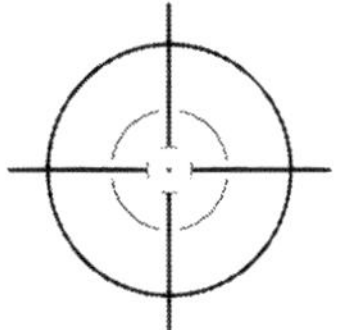

Chapter Fifteen

Casey Black walked around his captives, looking them over, trying to figure out why they were there at all. One smelled of lion and the other of wolf. Neither belonged at the hotel. They'd followed on the heels of a hit team that had shown, probably expecting an easy in and an easy out.

He laughed.

They'd gotten more than they'd bargained for.

Gus met Casey's gaze.

They aren't human, pushed Gus with his mind.

"I know," said Casey out loud.

The men on their knees, who had their hands bound behind their heads, shared a look that said they thought Casey was nuts. There were days he questioned his own sanity, so he didn't give a rat's ass what they thought of him. Besides, he was what the military had made him. A freak. Something that was against nature and the order of things. A man who was now part animal—part whatever else they did to him. Once, he'd been an elite soldier. And then he'd been their project, part of their experiment to make super soldiers. Now he was broken in their minds. An outcast, at first contained and locked away in what they wanted others to believe was a long-term care facility. It was a prison and then it had nearly been a tomb.

"The government sent them," stated Bill as he paced the edges of the room, shaking his head and moving in an erratic fashion—or as everyone else knew it as, Bill's norm. "The government has Laney and they sent the bully with pink hair to try to scare us. Sent the mean one too. So mean he has black eyes. But they didn't scare us, did they, Casey? We didn't run from the mechanical elephants in the jungle and we didn't run from pink hair or mean men."

Casey offered a warm grin. Bill had lost touch with anything close to reality years ago. Probably before he ever left the jungles of Vietnam. "No, Bill, they didn't scare us."

"Bag full of crazy shit in here," said the one with onyx eyes, who Bill had referred to as mean. "Mechanical elephants? That never happened. DARPA just considered it."

The man with pink hair tilted his head and lowered his gaze. "Actually…"

The dark eyed one groaned. "Figures. If you want a stupid plan, see them. I really hate scientists."

"You're married to one," reminded Pink Hair, an accent evident.

British?

The pink-haired guy was a Brit?

"Oh, right," said the other.

Bill stared at the men. "I was there. I saw 'em. I rode one."

Pink Hair seemed surprised. "You are the famed Wild Bill of Nam? The one who rode an out of control mechanical elephant for nearly ten minutes before they were able to disable it?"

"One in the same," said Bill with pride. "It

couldn't buck me. It didn't scare me and neither did the enemy. But the government lied. Told people it never sent the elephants. All they do is lie. They said it was the drugs making me see elephants that weren't there. But they were."

Pink Hair grinned. "They most certainly sent them. In fact, one is a lawn ornament for a friend of mine. He kept it as a souvenir."

"I knew they were real." Bill whistled and then pointed to the captive with pink hair. "You know where Laney is. We want our Laney back. Give us Laney or we shall give you death…or LSD. We'll do it, man. And you don't want the LSD. It makes you see all the shit you don't think is really there."

Gus stared off in the other direction but Casey knew the man was soaking in everything around him. That he saw more than most ever would or could. Whatever had been done to him by the scientists working for the government had left Gus with perceptive skills to a degree Casey had never seen before, and he'd seen a ton of weird shit. Gus didn't speak out loud, only via mental connections with other supernaturals.

Casey focused on the men. "Why did your strike team have a photo of Laney?"

He'd first assumed the hit team was there for him. That after all the years of staying off the grid, they had finally found him. When he'd finished dealing with them, he, Gus and Bill had searched the hit team, finding Laney's photo on one man.

They'd not been able to reach Laney on her cell since then. Worry settled into the pit of Casey's stomach. Laney was a sweet girl. She was young as far as supernaturals went, and hadn't a clue what she really was. She thought she was the caregiver to the men in the hotel, but in reality it was they who looked after her, a young, unmated supernatural female.

And now she was missing.

"Answer me!" shouted Casey.

The one with pink hair lifted a brow nonchalantly. "Why? You're not interested in the truth. You have your own reality and whatever I say you'll believe to be a lie."

"Say it anyways," demanded Casey.

"Laney, at last check, was alive and well and in the care of one of my men. Her fear for you lot brought us here. I see her concern was unwarranted," he said with a grunt.

Truth, pushed Gus at Casey.

The onyx-eyed one snorted. "Fucking never thought to mention we were walking into crazy-supernatural land."

"Are you telling me the hit team wasn't yours?" asked Casey, thankful Gus was near, because Casey wasn't sure he could be objective when it came to Laney. She was important to him. He'd been drawn to her and protective of her from the moment he found her on the streets—a punk-nosed girl barely in her teens at the time. It wasn't until tonight that he'd fully understood the reason why.

Pink Hair shot Casey a look that said *what do you think?*

Casey exhaled slowly, his body coiled with the need to strike someone, anyone, in regards to Laney being unreachable. "What did they want with her?"

"Can we please kill them now, Captain?" asked the one with dark eyes.

Bill stopped pacing and pointed at the man. "You're a big mean, meanie."

The man rolled his eyes. "That one's elevator stopped visiting all the floors."

Truth, pushed Gus.

Casey nearly laughed. Yes. It was true. Bill

was crazy but good-hearted.

"What does a hit team want with Laney," Casey pressed. "And what does a were-lion and a werewolf want with her?"

The men shared a look and then both of them locked gazes with him. The pink-haired one surveyed him, keeping his hands on his head. "What are you?"

Casey ignored the question. "Answer me."

"We want Laney. Laney. Laney," said Bill, chanting her name as he stomped around the room like a tin solider wound too tight. "Laney. Laney."

"For fuck's sake, Captain," said the dark-eyed one. "Two seconds, that's all it will take. Let me kill him."

The pink-haired man smiled. "No. James would not want harm to befall these men because they're important to the girl, and from what you told me, the girl is important to him."

"She better not be his mate." Duke groaned. "Look at the amount of crazy she brings to the table. Man, James will have this lot as in-laws."

Casey's gut clenched. "This James is who Laney met online? The one she had a date with tonight?"

Pink Hair nodded. "Though the date did not go as planned. Obviously."

The dark-eyed one stood and Casey made no move to attack the man again. Something deep down told him he may have been wrong about the two men before him. That they might not be the enemy after all. The man stretched and then tipped his head back and forth, his neck cracking.

"I'm too old for this shit," he said. He met Casey's gaze. "The little hacker and James have had the hots for each other since they started talking. They had a date tonight. It went sideways when a hit team showed. Probably from the same dicks who sent one here."

Casey gasped. "Laney?"

The guy lifted his shoulders. "I don't know. We came here at James's request to make sure you three crazy fucks weren't harmed and you all waylaid us." He shot an angry look at Bill. "And you are like a fucking monkey—jumping on me the way you did. I should have snapped your neck."

"Meanie," returned Bill, putting his thumbs in his ears and waving his fingers before blowing the man the raspberries.

The guy groaned. "And whatever you have going on in this room won't let either of us reach out and check on James or the girl."

Casey knew what he meant by reach out. He meant with his mind. Gus's telepathic skills far exceeded the average supernaturals, so he could still function normally within Casey's place, despite Casey turning on a makeshift L.A.R.D. device to block supernaturals from sending out mental signals to one another or receiving them. Casey had activated the machine right after the hit squad had attacked and been defeated.

"I fucking hate crazies," said the man. "Captain, reconsider letting me kill them. At least let me off the noisy one who acts like a monkey on a sugar high."

Bill stuck his tongue out at the man. "Meanie."

Truth, pushed Gus.

Casey glanced at the guy still on the floor. "Who are you with? What agency?"

The man stood and kept his hands on his head and Casey was pretty sure it was out of common courtesy and not because he couldn't break the cuffs. "*Quid pro quo.*"

Casey sighed. He'd get nothing more unless he offered something of value. "At one point, I had level-one clearance. I don't anymore. So, what are you? Shadow Agents?"

"Do we look like tortured souls who can't play nice with others?" snapped the dark-eyed one.

Casey nodded. "Yes."

"Duke," said Pink Hair. The man faced Casey. "PSI."

Casey tensed and weighed his options. He could run again and go to ground. He'd been doing it for decades. If he did, he'd never find out if Laney was well. And he'd have to leave Gus and Bill behind with PSI because neither of them could go on the run. They simply weren't equipped for it anymore in their advancing years and fragile mental states.

Once, Casey had been a mortal man. Not anymore. He'd not aged a day since he'd signed on to be part of the Immortal Ops Program. That had been just shy of a century ago. He'd been one of the first men to be brought, officially, into the program's folds.

He'd not been the last by any means.

If PSI was here, nosing around, it wouldn't be long before those who headed the I-Ops would realize who he was. An Outcast. A wanted fugitive in their minds. A failed attempt at greatness.

If I run, Laney could die.

She was important to him on a level he couldn't explain. She was like family and he'd been running a long time. Too long. He'd see her safe and then go.

He locked gazes with the captain. "Captain Casey Black, former Immortal Ops Agent."

The man narrowed his gaze and then sighed. "Outcast?"

Bill stopped stomping and demanding

Laney and put himself before Casey as if to protect him. While sweet, it was unwarranted. "Leave him alone. He's not broken. He's not damaged," said Bill.

Pink Hair lifted a hand. "Relax, small man," he said to Bill. "No harm will come to your friend. In fact, I know a group of men who have been looking for him."

Casey grunted. "A whole fucking government has been trying to track me and kill me."

"I'm Corbin Jones," the man said. "And information recently came to light about you and others like you, Captain. You need to understand something. The I-Ops themselves weren't part of what was done to you and the others like you."

"The rejects," offered Casey in a bitter tone.

"The men who went above and beyond for their country only to see that very country betray them," corrected Corbin. "The I-Ops and their colonel were only just given files on you all. They thought you all dead. All of us did."

"Then who has been hunting my kind?" asked Casey.

Duke grunted. "Fucking traitor dicks who we're gonna find and rip the heads off of. Nobody fucks with a soldier. Nobody."

Bill stuck his tongue out at the man again.

Casey looked to Gus, waiting for his thoughts on it all.

Gus met Casey's gaze, surprising him. "They speak the truth," said Gus, and Casey nearly lost his footing hearing the man speak out loud. "These men and their friends are not the enemy to you or us. But they do not understand the full layout of the war. They know only the recent battles. There are heads of the war who wear masks of bravery and honor, who pretend to be friend when they are foe. Who have secret agendas in line with those who seek world domination. They believe in their cause."

Corbin popped his cuffs off. "Let me guess, brain and telepathic testing subject?"

Casey nodded. "This is the first time I've heard him talk in all the years I've known him. He's always just communicated telepathically."

Gus stared out the window and Casey realized the man had said all he had to say on the matter. He focused his attention on Corbin. "You going to lock me up?"

"No. Your crime was trusting your country," returned the man. "Can you kindly stop doing whatever it is you're doing that has prevented us from linking with our teammates? We would like to check in and make sure..."

A big redheaded guy in a kilt came

bursting in, weapon in hand, pointing it at Casey. "Hands up!"

Casey rushed him and in the blink of an eye had him disarmed and the weapon trained on him. He prepared to fire.

"Casey, no!"

"Laney?" he asked, lowering the weapon, looking to the side as Laney came running in with a man wearing leather pants that he looked totally out of place in. Another man entered the room, and he too had on leather from head to toe, but he looked like he didn't mind it. Plus, with his long dark hair and eyeliner, it suited him.

"Why is Striker on the floor?" asked the newcomer.

Corbin snorted. "Because Casey put him there, Boomer. Welcome to the party. James, why are you wearing leather pants? You look like a deranged biker."

The one Casey had noted seemed uncomfortable in the leather pants blushed. "Might have had an incident with doing a full, uncontrolled change. Needed some clothes. Boomer had extras in the SUV."

Laney tossed her arms out and hugged Casey. "You're alive? I thought a hit team was going to come. Ohmygod, we should go in case they do. Bill? Gus?"

Bill smiled and waved. "Laney!"

Gus merely stared off into nowhere.

Laney teared up. "You're all okay. I'm so glad no one came to hurt you."

"Oh, a hit team showed," said Duke. "But the *Lone Wolf* here took them out all on his own. Handed us our asses too."

Corbin walked to the man on the floor in the kilt. "Handed Striker his as well. For that we are forever thankful to you."

"What the hell *are* you?" asked the man

called Striker. "Because yer nae human with that strength and speed."

"Don't be silly. Of course Casey is human," said Laney, releasing him and stepping back. It pained Casey to know there was trust in her voice and he'd violated it. He'd lied to her. She wasn't one to trust easily, and when she fully understood that he'd betrayed the trust he'd spent so long gaining, she would shut down on him. She'd never be able to wrap her mind around the true danger she was in.

Casey had been naïve at her age was well. He hadn't realized what lived among humans. What was really out there and what others were willing to do to protect those secrets. He knew the costs. He'd suffered them more than once and he wouldn't allow her to be hurt.

"Laney," he said. "We need to talk."

She motioned to James, paying Casey no mind. He knew her better than that. Knew she'd heard him but was trying to give him an out, a way to avoid hearing the truth. It was a truth she wasn't prepared to have confirmed.

"Casey, this is James, the guy I had a date with tonight and these are his friends. Something really bad is happening," she said.

Casey snorted. That was the understatement of the day. "I know."

She narrowed her gaze on him and then looked around the room. She was putting it all together. "What happened in here? It's trashed."

"Bad men came to kill *our* Laney," said Bill, patting his knees and then clapping his hands as if playing a game of patty cake all by his lonesome. He'd been known to do stranger things. "Casey and his wolf said no. His wolf came out and it let them know that our Laney was not to be harmed. Nope."

"Casey and his wolf?" Laney paled and

then bent forward, looking as if she might be sick. James moved closer to her and rubbed her back. She touched his thigh and Casey considered forcing the man to get the hell away from Laney. Mating energy coated the air around them and Casey's overdeveloped senses picked up on it right away.

Fuck.

He did not want her mated to a PSI Operative. A supernatural male who lived a normal life was his choice—not that he got to make one. Destiny had other plans. And she seemed to need his comfort at the moment so he allowed it.

"Casey is a shifter, isn't he?" she asked James.

James's gaze met Casey's and there was compassion reflected back. "Sweeting."

Casey sighed. The moment of truth was upon him. "Yes, Laney. I am."

She looked up at him. "All the stories you told me about the government and the experiments on humans to make them into animal-like soldiers, it wasn't just theories you heard, was it? You weren't telling me stories you made up. Were you?"

He shook his head. "I lived it."

We should go, pushed Gus. *Now.*

Casey looked to Corbin. "Gus says we need to leave. Believe me, he's right. He must sense something big coming."

Laney frowned. "Gus doesn't talk."

"He does, but not in ways most can hear, hon," Casey said, hating that they'd kept the truth from her. They'd only wanted to keep her safe. The less she knew the safer she would have been.

Damn her curiosity.

She gasped. "Danger? Someone shouted *danger* in my head earlier. It was Gus, wasn't it?"

Casey shrugged. "He might have. Even I'm not clear how he does what it is he does. I do know if he says we should go, he's not playing around."

"Let's take this show on the road," said Duke. "I fucking hate standing around waiting to be attacked again. We can debrief somewhere safe. Can we leave the little loud one?"

"Bill comes with us," stated Casey clearly. "As does Gus. I want them safe."

"Laney needs to rest," said James, drawing Laney closer to him. "She's been through a lot and I want her checked over before we do anything else."

"I'm fine," said Laney.

It pained Casey to tell her what he'd had to do. He knew it would upset her. "Laney, your computer system."

She blinked up at him. "What about it?"

Bill lifted his hands in the air. "Casey was a bad, bad boy. He broke it."

Laney's eyes widened. "What?"

Casey exhaled slowly. "When I realized the hit team was looking for you and not me, I did what needed to be done to protect you. I know how much that computer meant to you but, Laney, the information you'd been digging for, it nearly got you killed."

She said nothing as she turned, taking James's hand in hers as she headed for the door. Casey tried to follow, but James glanced over his shoulder and shook his head, as if sensing it wasn't the time.

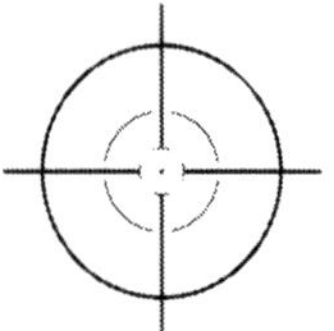

Chapter Sixteen

Bertrand snarled as he held one of his pets by the throat. "Tell me again how they escaped?"

The hybrid, a mix of man, bat, vampire and tiger, shook its head as best it could with Bertrand's claws biting into its flesh. "We don't know, sir. We sent a team. We found a cleanup crew in the alley, disposing of our team's bodies."

Bertrand's vision narrowed as red filtered into the rims of his view. "You and the others are weak. You let a hacker and an injured shifter bring you all down."

"No, sir. No. I'm sure they had help," the hybrid said, pleading with his eyes for mercy.

It wasn't in Bertrand to grant anyone leniency. He twisted quickly, tearing the hybrid's throat out and flinging it aside, his gaze finding the row of other hybrids, none saying a word. They knew he possessed the power. That without Bertrand they would not continue to receive the injections they were now dependent upon for their survival.

"What of the other team?" asked Bertrand, fire in his belly. "The one sent to the location the girl lived?"

"Dead," whispered one of the men. "All dead."

This was what he got for dealing with the bottom of barrel in regards to trained professionals. If he was ever going to get Gisbert and the other heads of the Corporation to see him as a leader, he had to act now. He couldn't take this defeat lying down.

"If you want something done, you have to do it yourself." With that, he clicked his fingers for a towel, waiting before one appeared, and then wiped his hands. It was time he took matters into his own hands. He would pay Hagen a visit and he would get what he needed once and for all.

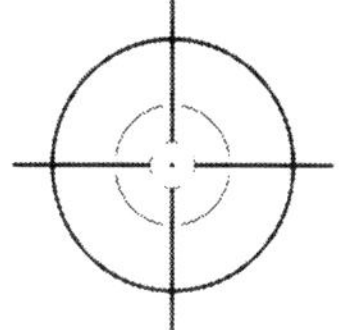

Chapter Seventeen

James took the now-cooled mug of tea from Laney's hand and pushed her damp hair from her shoulder. This woman had seen him at his worst—eating hybrids while stuck in a bloodlust shifter state—and she still somehow managed to see something good in him. He couldn't understand why. She had agreed to come to his home with him, rather than a safe house. Even after all she'd seen and been through.

The worst first date ever.

Here she was, in his home, on his sofa, her smell coating everything, and he loved it. Shame pushed through him. She'd had a hell of a night and *he* was thinking of how good she smelled.

They'd stopped first at his lab, where he'd looked her over, making sure she wasn't harmed. He'd also taken samples of her blood and had another, trusted doctor at PSI, working to see what he could find. Patterson swore he'd call the minute he learned anything conclusive. James had already phoned him twice, seeing if he could speed up the process. PSI labs were equipped with technologies other labs, even top-notch ones, weren't. Things that seemed more sci-fi than real. A perk of the job.

If only the damn job would call him and full-out confirm his woman was supernatural and enough supernatural for him to be able to claim her without it being the end of her. James had seen it happen to men before—men who went against what nature ruled and decided to try to make a life and a family with a woman who lacked paranormal qualities and certain levels of supernatural in her line.

It always ended bad.

Very bad.

"Casey, Bill and Gus are okay?" she asked for probably close to the tenth time since they'd parted ways at headquarters with them. She sipped the tea and he was happy she was finally putting something in her stomach.

James nodded. "They are. Bill and Gus are going to be spending some time in a halfway house PSI actually owns and operates. It's for supernaturals. And there are people there who are trained to help with their special circumstances."

"They'll be okay there?" she asked.

"Yes."

"And Casey?"

James sighed. "He was offered a chance to stay on and help at PSI. But, Laney, you need to know something."

She looked up at him, mug in hand. "What?"

"Corbin called when you were showering," he said, wishing he didn't have to be the bearer of bad news. "Duke and Striker left Casey in one of the extra sleeping quarters there, and when they went in to check on him after his supposed shower, he was gone."

"Gone? Like vanished?"

James nodded.

"He just walked out of a secret government facility without anyone noticing?" she asked, doubt on her face.

"Yes. He did."

The edges of her lips curled upwards and her mood seemed to lighten somewhat. "He outfoxed *the Man*."

James grunted. "I guess he did."

"I never knew he was a shifter," she said. "I should have seen it. He shouldn't have felt like he had to hide that from me. I'd have understood. It wouldn't have changed how I saw him."

He knew she would have understood. She'd been accepting of his own wolf. More than most would be in her place.

James pushed her damp hair over her shoulder. She was punishing herself for something out of her control. She hadn't known the truth about Casey, but Casey kept it from her. The man had learned long ago how to hide what he was. Laney couldn't kick herself for not figuring it out. "He cares for you. He waited until he knew you were safe before he vanished. He could have left at any moment, but he made sure you and your other friends were in good hands."

She twisted slightly and the shirt she had on, which was one of James's dress shirts, pulled to one side, showing the mounds of her breasts. His entire body had been on fire since he'd laid eyes on her. The cold shower he'd taken while she was taking a long, hot warm one in his master bath had done nothing to temper his cock and its single-minded focus. Seeing the pale globes of her breasts, there, so close, knowing they were bare under the thin material, nearly pushed James over the edge of sexual sanity.

He put his hands on his legs, trying to think on anything but Laney's breasts. As he rubbed his palms, trying to get the sweat from them, he realized something. He'd not limped once since he'd fully shifted. In fact, nothing on him hurt.

Well, unless he counted his dick.

That hurt like a motherfucker.

It wanted in her. Wanted to know what pleasures her body could bring.

He tipped his head back, swallowing hard.

You will not take advantage of her in this state, he chanted. *You will not take advantage of her. You will not…*

She put her hand over his, her fingertips skimming his inner thigh.

Fuck. Fuck. Fuck. You will not take advantage of her.

He jerked and sat up some, hoping to keep from both coming and ignoring his inner voice.

"Thank you for saving my life," she said sweetly, the innocence in her voice making him feel like an even bigger douche.

"All in a day's work," he mused, earning him a slight smile from her. She'd been quiet since they'd left the hotel, barely uttering a word as James checked her in his lab, and saying nothing on the ride to his house. "How are you holding up with all of this?"

"What's a mate?" she asked, surprising him to the point he actually, for a brief moment, forgot about his seemingly endless hard-on.

"Why do you want to know?"

She handed him the mug of tea and faced him more. "Because your friends said something in the alley. They said I was your mate. I want to know what that means."

James nearly crushed the mug. He had to try to gently set it on the side table when all he wanted to do was permit his wolf up to do what it had wanted to do from the word go.

Claim the woman before him.

"W-what, exactly, happened?" he asked, needing to be sure and that his wires weren't crossed.

"Striker said he smelled Fae on me. Then Boomer said he smelled panther and then they both sniffed me like basset hounds before announcing that I was your mate. Your woman."

Closing his eyes a second, James let out a long, slow breath, the tension and fear of doing something regrettable leaving him. He wasn't mis-wired. He wasn't nuts. His body had been doing what it was supposed to do—try to get him to claim his mate.

His woman.

Mine.

He didn't fear the word anymore or what it implied.

The burning need to wait for medical clarification eased. His brothers-in-arms would never say that if it wasn't true. They'd never lead him astray. They knew how important and special it was to find one's mate. And both liked Laney—a lot. Striker had even taken to calling her Punky at headquarters. That was right after he tried to get her to trick out his online profile page so that it would auto growl and howl at women who were hot.

Thankfully, she'd declined to help him.

James touched her cheek, his feelings for her growing by the second. They'd spent a week connecting intimately through conversation and then an evening together, fighting for their lives all the while the attraction growing.

It's more than merely attraction, he corrected. *It's love. As it is between a mated pair.*

"It means you were created for me. A perfect match according to the supernatural world. The woman who is meant to be my wife."

She frowned and stared at her lap.

She didn't want him. The knowledge cooled him and he slid away from her, giving her space. He stood slowly. It hurt to be rejected by the woman he knew in his bones was his, but he understood. He wouldn't force her to be with him, even though, by archaic laws that still existed in the supernatural community, he could.

That wasn't James.

"I'll phone Corbin and arrange for you to be placed in protective custody. I understand you don't want to be here with me."

"What?" she asked, confusion knitting her brow. "Are you sending me away?"

"Gods no," he said. "I thought you wanted to leave."

"Why would you think that?"

He sat again and offered a slight smile.

"Because I can't read your mind."

"So you claim," she teased, easing closer to him, her hand returning to his sweatpants-covered thigh. It felt damn good to be out of the leather pants. They'd been very constricting. When she was showering in his master bathroom, he'd used the guest bath and cleaned up as well, needing to wash the scents of the alley off him.

"Laney, my body sees you as its mate," he said. He put his hand over hers. "And if Striker and Boomer both sensed it too, I believe it's true. That being said, I know you've never been with a man before and that we've only just officially met, and that this was a horrible date night."

"Doc Wolf," she said softly.

"Yes?"

"Shut up and kiss me."

He paused. "I want to. Ohgods, do I want

to. But, Laney, my control around you is shaky. If I kiss you and you're in just that shirt and I'm in just these sweatpants, this will go too far."

"Okay," she said, and before he knew it she was pressed against him, on her knees, her hands finding his face. "Hagen, look at me. Please."

He did.

"You saved my life tonight," she said, looking so incredibly young with her makeup washed off that James held more guilt about their age difference.

He nodded slightly.

Laney's lips met his and her kiss was tender and short. Too short. The wolf in him roared to life, wanting more. So did the man. He tossed his arms out, his hands going to the top of the back of his sofa in an attempt to keep from yanking the gorgeous woman near him onto his lap.

Where he wanted her to be more than anything.

She crawled up and over his lap, her wet hair falling onto his bare shoulders. He'd been so concerned about her that he'd tossed on a pair of sweatpants and nothing more after his shower. He wished he'd put on armor, because his cock was rock-fucking-hard and there was no hiding it from her.

"Laney?" he asked, his voice strained.

She settled herself on his lap and then kissed him again. He held so tight to the sofa back he thought he might actually rip the thing off the base. Pulling his mouth back, he broke the kiss, only to keep from flipping her onto her back and driving into her.

She wasn't ready for that.

Her dark gaze searched his face. "I want you, Hagen. I want all of you."

She is a virgin who has been through a traumatic experience, he reminded himself. His cock throbbed and twitched against her mound. It, apparently, couldn't give a shit.

Laney reached down between them and boldly put her hand on his distended flesh. James sucked in a sharp breath and jolted with a start beneath her.

"Laney, please. You don't want this. You'll regret it," he said.

She kissed him again, her tongue artfully easing around his as she rubbed his clothed cock. When he realized she was undoing the dress shirt she now wore with her free hand, James considered bolting and running, locking the door behind him. If only to save her from his lack of willpower.

Damn if his body didn't refuse to budge.

He ground his hips upwards, taking control of the kiss. Laney reached for his arms.

Her breasts, covered only by thin material, pressed to his chest. He nearly came then and there. It had been a long time for him.

Too fucking long.

He'd never last if she kept this up.

Her fingers found the waistband of his sweatpants and she met his gaze, slowing the kiss, giving him a questioning look. "Am I hurting you?"

"I'm dying a little inside as I try to keep from taking advantage of you, but other than that—" He squirmed under her, his cock painfully hard. "—I'm good."

"It looks like I'm hurting you," she said, her free hand coming to his cheek. "Hagen, if I am, tell me."

"Don't stop," he found himself saying.

She eased open his sweatpants, and the moment her hand wrapped around the head of his cock, James stopped trying to restrain himself and gave in, his hands going to the dress shirt she wore. He paused, his breathing harsh. "Yes or no, Laney?"

"Yes," she whispered a second before he tore the shirt open, sending buttons flying everywhere.

He didn't care that he'd just ruined one of his shirts. All he cared about were her breasts as they spilled forth. They were just the right size, filling his hands as he cupped them, his mouth making love to hers. He wanted to drive into her, take what he wanted, but he couldn't.

She'd never been with a man before.

He needed to be gentle.

James stood, lifting Laney up with him and turning her, placing her on the sofa. He stared down at her there, the shirt open wide, her breasts exposed to him. His gaze went to her black panties and a wolfish grin spread over his face as he lowered himself, going to his knees before the sofa. He traced a line down between her breasts and over her stomach before he reached her panties. With a slight tug he lowered them, his gaze never leaving hers as he dipped his head, inhaling the sweet scent of her cream.

The woman smelled divine.

He worked her panties off her with ease, casting them aside, his head returning to between her legs. He opened them more and nibbled lightly on her inner thighs.

She ran her hands through the top of his hair as he lowered his mouth to her slit. He flicked his tongue over her clit and she jerked under him, making him smile as she began to pant with each swipe. He pressed a finger to her wet core but he didn't push it in, not yet. He waited and she reached down, grabbing his hand, shaking her head.

He assumed she wanted it to end. His dick wanted to howl with frustration. Stopping nearly killed him, but being a man of honor, he moved to stand and give her the space she needed.

"No," she said. "Don't go."

Confused, he tipped his head to the side. "Sweeting?"

"I want your…" She looked at his groin. "…to be what takes my virginity, not your finger. You."

Hot need slammed into him. He had to strain to talk and not allow his mouth to shift shape. "No, let me get you ready for me."

"Hagen, please."

Dammit. He couldn't tell her no and mean it.

My woman has me tied around her little finger.

He'd been so swept up in meeting her and in worrying about her safety that he'd not really had a moment to process what he knew was true. As the reality of it sank in and James thought harder about events, he took a giant step back.

"Holy crapola," he said, echoing the words she'd used before.

Laney propped herself on her elbows, looking even more sexy, if that were even possible. "Hagen?"

"We need to stop," he said, wanting to do anything but.

"Oh, we need to get this darn show on the road, bucko," she said, reaching for him.

James went to her and bent over her, her smell filling his head. "Laney, you don't understand. I think...I think you're my mate. Actually, I more than think you are. I know that doesn't mean anything to you, but to me, to others like me, it's a huge deal. It means the chances of me claiming you, even if you don't want me to, are high. It's been over a century since I've been with a woman, and I know for a fact I won't be able to stop myself with you."

She blinked up at him. "How friggin' old are you?"

He bit the corner of his lip. "Old."

"Like Dracula kind of old?" she asked.

As much as he disliked being associated with a vampire, even a fictional one, he understood her line of questioning. "No. Not that old."

"But old enough to have a century under your belt?" she questioned.

"Uh, more than one," he said softly.

She stared at his chest. "What does claiming entail? Does it leave you buried deep in me? If so, I say we do it."

Fuck!

"Laney."

She gave him a pointed stare. "LabLupus,

either get over here now and do me or so help me God I will walk out of here and never speak to you again."

James couldn't help but smile as he slid his sweatpants off. Laney's eyes widened as she stared at his long, thick cock as it bobbed before her, nearly eye level with the position she was in.

"Oh, is that going to work?"

He grunted. "It's been a long time, but I'm pretty sure he remembers how this goes."

She blew out a long breath, sending strands of her dark hair flying. "No. I mean, will that fit in me?"

He nearly laughed. "Let me get you ready, sweeting."

She reached for him and he moved up and over her partially, his lips returning to hers. His intention was to kiss her, get her body to relax some, and then to slide down the length of her and use his tongue and fingers to prepare her for sex.

Laney clearly had other intentions. She reached between them and grabbed his cock roughly, jerking on it, lining it up with her pussy. She was fast, too fast for him as she pressed herself up, causing his cockhead to spear her entrance. Hot, tight, wet pleasure greeted him and he nearly lost control then and there. He met with resistance and lost ability to act like a rational man. Instead, he drove into her tight channel, pushing in, going balls deep, making her cry out in his arms.

The realization he had hurt her hit him hard.

James froze.

Laney clawed at his upper arms. "More. Don't stop. Keep going."

His lips found hers and he smiled quickly, his cock more than happy to keep going. He pumped in and out of her, slow at first, giving her the time he should have before to adjust to his size. When she began to counter his thrusts, James sped things up, pounding into her harder and faster.

He'd never last like this. He'd never make it. She felt too good and it had been too long.

He was so worried about coming before she did that he didn't notice his wolf creeping up on him. James never realized until it was too late, until he was slamming into his woman, his teeth now lengthened, his wolf dancing on the surface. His gaze locked onto her shoulder.

"Mine!" he growled out, his head going down quickly, his teeth sinking into her tender flesh. Her blood filled his mouth and he tried to beat his wolf down, to make it stop. He couldn't. His body was on autopilot as he thrust into his woman, claiming her fully.

She held tight to him, her nails biting into his skin. He felt her channel tightening around his cock and then releasing, repeating the actions again, and he knew she'd hit her zenith. He pushed in hard and deep, stilling, her blood easing down his throat as his seed jetted into her.

"Yes, yours," she whispered against his ear.

The minute she spoke the words, it felt as if some unseen force was in the room with them, weaving threads between them, connecting them for all eternity. James managed to tear his mouth from her shoulder and looked down, realizing what he'd done. In stunned horror, he nearly pulled out and left her body, but Laney locked her legs around him, countering his moves, her pussy milking the seed from his body.

She licked her fingertips and James realized his blood was on them from where she'd scratched him during sex. "Mine," she said, her eyes flashing with a burst of colors.

Fuck DNA samples. He had proof. She was plenty supernatural if her eyes could do that.

"Yours," he said, nodding and then lowering his mouth and licking her shoulder where he'd bitten her. The bite healed instantly and James's cock, which should have been spent and in need of a break between rounds, remained rock hard as he kept going, kept moving in and out of his mate.

His wife.

Smiling, he found her lips and kissed her, her arms wrapping around his neck as she returned each swipe of his tongue with her own.

Wow. I got my V-card punched by the hottest, hung werewolf, ever.

James stilled, Laney's voice ringing through his head. His lips shook against her mouth. V-card? Hung?

His wife was something indeed and he planned to punch her card over and over again all night long.

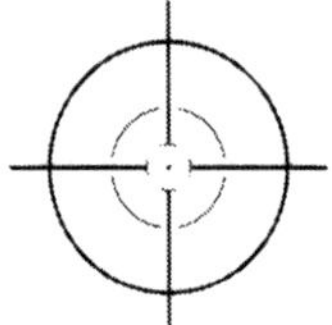

Chapter Eighteen

Laney rolled onto her side and looked at Hagen as he slept. He was gorgeous and she could have sworn the man had bulked up more in the three days they'd spent holed up in his home, learning one another's body completely. She traced a finger over the hard planes of his torso and his eyes snapped open, his green gaze looking hungry for more sex.

She giggled. "Oh no. No more of that right now. I think you've had enough."

He rolled up and over her so fast that she gasped. Her legs opened for him, already trained as to how to respond to his nearness. His cockhead pushed against her core. "I'll never have enough."

She touched his stubble-covered chin. "Hagen, we should get up. Don't you have to work or something?"

He laughed. "Yes, but they've given me time off for my honeymoon."

She licked her lips. "I still can't believe you're my husband. It's so weird."

He kissed her, his cock easing into her slowly. He settled in, balls deep, but didn't move. "It's perfect. It's not weird."

Yes, it's weird.

No, she heard his voice in her mind. *It's not.*

She gasped and sat up, knocking heads with him, making him withdraw from her body. "Holy crapola, you lied. You can totally read my mind!"

Laughing, Hagen touched her forehead. "Are you okay?"

She swatted his hand away. "Dude, you read my mind. That is it. I'm wearing a tin foil hat to bed. Period."

He gave her a serious expression. "Laney, I didn't lie before. I couldn't read it then. I think my head was a little screwed up with anxiety. It wasn't until I fully claimed you that I was able to read your thoughts."

She pursed her lips. "Really?"

He nodded. "Really."

She pulled a pillow up and used it to cover the front of her body. "Can I read yours?"

"With some practice, yes," he said.

"That makes it cooler."

He grinned and reached for her, his fingers skimming her nipple. "I want to be in you."

"You always want to be in me."

"I know," he said. "Life is good. I get to stay in bed with the woman I love."

Laney eased back and stared at him. "What?"

Hagen sat up more, his cock, long, hard and thick, sticking up from his neatly maintained thatch of hair between his legs. "I'm not sure what you're asking me, sweeting."

"You love me?"

He gave her the "you simple sweet woman" look again. She hated that look. "Laney, of course I love you."

"Oh." She blushed and then tried to slide off the bed.

He caught her around the waist, her back now to his front, his cock pushing against her thigh. "Do you love me?"

She started to say she wasn't sure, that she'd only known him a short time, but that wasn't what came out. "Yes. I love you, Hagen."

He kissed her earlobe. "I can sense your fear of this. It's new. It's scary and you don't know how to process those feelings."

She nodded.

"It's new to me too, but its not scary, Laney. It's the single greatest thing that has ever happened to me," he said, easing her against him more, his cock head digging and probing at her wet slit from behind. She knew he was drawn to her ass and she yelped, fearful he'd just do it.

He chuckled. "You're not quite ready for that yet, sweeting."

She relaxed.

He continued to push at her pussy with his

cock from behind as he held her body to his. "I've lived a long life. A part of it in the last century hasn't been great. And a month ago I was ready to check out, quit life and never look back."

She tensed, her nails digging into his arm. She knew from talking more in-depth with him since their mating that he'd been held by the Corporation for almost a year and tortured. That he'd really only been free a few weeks. She couldn't imagine her life without him, without meeting him, without mating to him and without falling in love with him.

"Hagen," she said, her voice low as she rocked her body back and onto his cock, letting it spear her pussy sweetly. Pleasure settled over her, her lower body tightening with anticipation.

Hagen began to move slowly, easing out of her before pushing in again, his mouth on her neck as he nibbled lightly on the flesh just under her ear. He increased his pace and Laney lost herself in the bliss of it all, the feel of her husband deep in her, the sense of her pending culmination.

"Hagen!"

Her body shattered around his and he thrust in deep, erupting in her, filling her with his hot seed. He put his lips to her ear once more. "Laney Hagen, I love you."

She liked the sound of his last name being hers. "Love you too, Doc Wolf."

"Isn't this touching," a deep voice said from the doorway of their bedroom.

In the blink of an eye, Hagen was gone from her body and over her, never touching her as he leapt at the intruder, growling, shifting in midair. There was a crashing noise behind Laney and she realized it was the window breaking inwards.

Fear slammed through her and she grabbed the sheet just as something snatched hold of her ankle, ripping her off the bed.

"Now, now, Hagen," said the man from the doorway. "Temper, temper. My man has your woman. Make a move to harm me and she will be dead before you can turn around."

Laney held the sheet against her naked form as something hot breathed down on her cheek, its grip iron-clad.

Hagen stood naked and unabashed in the center of their room, his claws out as he glared at the ugliest man she'd never seen. The man's beady eyes seemed full of wicked glee. His very presence made her shudder.

"Bertrand," Hagen snarled.

Bertrand entered the room more and tossed a pair of silver shackles at Hagen's feet. "Put them on," he commanded.

Hagen didn't move.

Bertrand snapped his fingers and whatever was holding Laney jerked hard on her neck. She cried out, pain moving over her.

Hagen stiffened. “Stop! I’ll put them on.”

Laney had heard of Bertrand, of what he’d done to Hagen. Of what he’d wanted to do even. The more she looked at the ugly man, the more her anger rose. Time seemed to slow as Laney watched her husband bending to retrieve the shackles. He put one on his left wrist and then the other on his right.

“Leave my wife out of this,” he said, sounding defeated.

Bertrand eyed him, his gaze centering on Hagen’s exposed body. “I am going to enjoy you.”

“Like hell you are, weasel-dick,” Laney shouted, her rage consuming her at the same moment something extremely hot did as well. What was that buzzing? It was so loud, it drowned out everything else in the room. The urge to strike out came over her and she did. She elbowed the thing holding her, unconcerned if the sheet stayed up to cover her or not. The thing went backwards and she twisted. She was about to lift her hands to strike him when suddenly a red dot appeared on his forehead. Blood seeped from it.

It took Laney a minute to realize the hybrid had been shot in the forehead. She didn't do it. Hagen didn't do it. Who did it?

She grabbed the sheet from the floor and spun, expecting to see Striker or another of Hagen's teammates coming to the rescue. Instead, she watched in awe as he husband snapped the shackles binding him and charged Bertrand. He began to beat the ever-loving shit out of the guy with his bare, unshifted hands.

Casey was suddenly there, pulling at Hagen, trying to force him back to no avail.

Casey yanked harder. "I can't question a dead man, Hagen."

"He attacked my woman!" yelled Hagen between blows.

"Hagen," Laney said softly, bringing his attack to a grinding halt. "No more."

He let Bertrand's limp head thump to the floor before standing, still not really caring that he was naked. He faced Casey, who was dressed head-to-toe in black ops gear. "You're who I've sensed shadowing the place the last few days. I thought it was Boomer or Striker trying to be helpful."

Casey shrugged and then looked to Laney. "You okay?"

She held the sheet around her and nodded. "Yes."

"Nicely done on finally letting your magik loose, hon," said Casey.

Laney tipped her head. "My what?"

He pursed his lips. "Magik. It was dormant in you, Laney. The shifter in you is diluted to a degree that you have increased strength and speed but you won't be able to ever shift forms."

"Her eyes do," said Hagen, tossing her one of the nightgowns he'd had delivered for her. He'd had a wardrobe arrive within twenty-four hours of her arrival. He'd also had a super nice computer system delivered.

Laney caught the nightgown and slipped it over her head, her gaze going to Casey. "I thought I'd never see you again."

"Hagen knew better, didn't you?" he asked of Hagen. "Figure it out yet?"

Hagen's jaw tightened as he grabbed a pair of boxers from his dresser and slipped them on, walking over and kicking Bertrand once more for good measure. "Patterson from PSI called me yesterday with the results of her tests. He consulted with Dr. Green out of I-Ops."

Casey glanced in Laney's direction. "I didn't know they'd use the samples they took from all of us to do what they did. I didn't know the samples would end up in the hands of monsters. Please know that."

Laney wasn't following.

Hagen sighed. "The Asia Project, Laney. Casey is trying to tell you that some of his DNA was used by the assholes who ran the Asia Project."

"And?" she asked, not following.

Hagen stood tall. "Some of his DNA was used in your creation."

She stilled. "Is he my dad?"

Casey laughed. "No. But, I'm pretty much family to you. Explains why I was drawn to you in a protective manner when I first crossed paths with you."

"And why you stayed with me all those years," she said, realizing he'd been on the run a long time before her.

Casey nodded.

Hagen watched him. "When did you figure it out?"

"After the hit squad came to the hotel. When I was accessing Laney's computer system and reading her files. I recognized my own DNA sequence listed in the samples used in her creation."

"Are you going to vanish again?" she asked, sorrow coating her words.

He fell silent for what felt like forever. "Laney, there is something else."

She crossed the room and put her hand out to her husband. He took it and pulled her close. "What?" she asked.

"I know you've been trying to reach Harmony, but that you haven't been able to," he said.

Laney nodded. "I'm going to go to her house in the morning and beat down the front gates if I have to. I can't believe how hard it's been to sync back up with her now that my computer system is down."

Casey stiffened. "Laney, you haven't been able to reach her for a reason."

Laney's gut tightened. "No. She's not dead. Tell me she's not dead."

"Gus contacted me," said Casey. "The night of the attacks, while we were at PSI headquarters."

Laney remained silent.

"Gus was headed to a safe house and he reached out to me mentally, warning me that the blonde one was in harm's way." Casey lowered his gaze. "That she was at the hotel and that more bad men had come."

Laney had to work hard to get what he

was saying. Her gaze went to Bertrand, who was still breathing, but out cold in a bloody heap on the floor. "Oh gods, he went to the hotel after we all left, didn't he? He did something to Harmony—that is why you stopped Hagen from killing him. You said you can't question a dead man."

Hagen pulled her tighter to him. "Sweeting."

Casey looked pained as he spoke. "I tried to get there in time. I did. I was too late. They'd taken her by then. And, Laney, you never told me you had a backup system."

Laney squeezed Hagen's hand. "It wasn't as powerful as the other. It was just in the event of my death system."

Casey stared at her. "Harmony did something from it. She published something to the internet before she was captured." Casey looked away. "Laney, your sites and the internet forums are full of people who now believe what you proposed—that supernaturals are real."

Her goal at one point had been to expose the truth. That was before she knew and understood what was at stake. She cupped her mouth with her free hand. "No."

"I've got friends working on countering it all, on making it look bogus," he said. "They're good. We might be able to make this look like the Roswell."

Laney lowered her gaze. "My best friend might be dead and I exposed the secret of supernaturals to the world."

Casey exhaled. "On a good note, most of the people on the boards you run are loons."

She stared up at her husband, wondering how angry he was with her. He bent his head and kissed the tip of her nose. "Go shower. Casey and I will clean up this mess and see to it Bertrand is transported to a PSI holding facility where we can interview him."

"If by interview you mean cut his balls off if he doesn't tell you were Harmony is, then I support this decision," she said.

He grinned. "That's my girl. Now scoot."

"I'm sorry."

"I love you. Get your ass in the shower."

She nodded and pushed a smile to her face. The road they were walking together wasn't going to be easy. Not by a long shot, but at least she had a man who loved her unconditionally by her side.

"Laney," said Casey. "I'll find her and I'll bring her back safe."

Laney choked up. "You can't stand her."

He snorted. "Hon, there is a fine line between love and hate."

What was he trying to say?

It dawned on her and she teared up. "You

find her and you bring her back to us, okay?"

"I will."

She touched Hagen's arm on her way to the bathroom. "Kick that sick bastard Bertrand in the nuts at least once for me, okay?"

"Will do," he said.

I love you, she pushed with her mind, wondering if he'd get the message.

I love you too, sweeting.

THE END

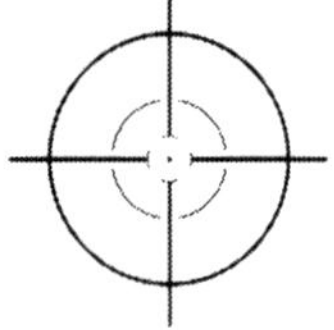

Note to readers: Want to read Casey and Harmony's story? Look for the *Immortal Outcast Series Novella: Broken Communication.* Part of the Immortal Ops and PSI-Ops World.

About the Author, Mandy M. Roth

Mandy M. Roth grew up fascinated by creatures that go bump in the night. From the very beginning, she showed signs of creativity —writing, painting, telling scary stories that left her little brother afraid to come out from under his bed. Combining her creativity with her passion for the paranormal has left her banging on the keyboard into the wee hours of the night.

She's a self-proclaimed Goonie, loves 80s music and movies and wishes leg warmers would come back into fashion. She also thinks the movie *The Breakfast Club* should be mandatory viewing for...okay, everyone. When she's not dancing around her office to the sounds of the 80s or writing books, she can be found designing book covers for New York publishers, small presses, and indie authors.

Mandy writes for The Raven Books, Samhain Publishing, Ellora's Cave Publishing, Harlequin Spice, Pocket Books and Random House/Virgin/Black Lace. Mandy also writes under the pen names Reagan Hawk, Mandy Balde, Rory Michaels and Kennedy Kovit.

To learn more about Mandy, please visit http://www.mandyroth.com or send an email to mandy@mandyroth.com.

For latest news about Mandy's newest releases subscribe to her newsletter

http://www.mandyroth.com/newsletter.htm

Mandy M. Roth, Online

Mandy loves hearing from readers and can be found interacting on social media.

(copy & paste links into your browser window)

Website: http://www.MandyRoth.com

Blog: http://www.MandyRoth.com/blog

The Raven Books: http://www.TheRavenBooks.com

Facebook: http://www.facebook.com/AuthorMandyRoth

Twitter: @MandyMRoth

Book Release Newsletter: mandyroth.com/newsletter.htm

(Newsletters: I do not share emails and only send newsletters when there is a new release/ contest/ or sales)

The Raven Books' Complimentary Material

The following material is free of charge. It will never affect the price of your book.

King of Prey: A Bird Shifter Novel by Mandy

M. Roth

In a place where realms combine and portals open passages to the unknown, a prophecy speaks of fertility being restored to King Kabril's people through the taking of his mate.

The prophecy neglects to mention she lacks something vital to his kind--wings. Kabril, king of the *Buteos Regalis,* has no interest in taking a human mate. His kind believe humans are dirty, vile creatures who rely on machines to lift them into the air. The last place he wants to go in search of his mate is the realm of Earth, but he's left no choice.

Never did he expect to find love on a planet with one moon, people who lack wings and a stubborn vixen who makes his heart soar. When he does, he fears the truth about who and what he truly is will steal it away. Little does he know his enemies fully intend on doing the taking.

Excerpt from King of Prey: A Bird Shifter Novel Book One by Mandy M. Roth

Chapter One

Accipitridae Realm

"King Kabril, you cannot stand idly by while your people cry out for you to lead. Our race will not survive unless you take a wife. The mating magik that governs our lands will not grant established unions the blessing of children if the leader himself refuses to sire offspring," Sachin said, his words the truth. As head advisor to the king he was afforded the opportunity to speak freely where others were not. It was a privilege Kabril was fast beginning to suspect needed to be revoked.

"You know the laws, the way of the land and the demands you must meet as king. The time has come, my lord. This can wait no longer. The people of Accipitridae need you to act now."

Though Sachin's words were the truth, they were not what Kabril wanted to hear. No. He much rather preferred hearing all was well and that none of the people under his rule were troubled. Of course, those moments were few and far between of late. The rumbles of pending war continued to make their way through the kingdom. Now was not the time for foolishness or for stopping everything to heed the warnings of those who did not leave their chambers.

Ever.

Seers and the Oracle.

He grunted. He had no time time for prophecy.

It had been a good long while since his people had been in full-scale war. Yes, they had the occasional run-in with the enemy, but nothing epic. Too long for some to remember the horrors of it, yet not long enough for others to be afforded the chance to forget.

Kabril was one of the men who could not forget. He did not want a repeat, nor did he want his people's moods soured because he was refusing to do what was required of him as king. Gods be damned if what they required didn't go against his very nature.

Select a wife.

Settle upon only one woman—forever?

Absurd.

Truly, he would have thought it a trick of the Oracle had so many not stood behind the words.

Foolish words.

Sighing, Kabril leaned back on his throne

and stared into the reflective mixture Sachin held in the bowl. He ran his fingers over the scrolled armrest and glanced down at the carved hawks. A slow smile caused by pride moved over his face. Pride in his people, their traditions and their beliefs, even though those very beliefs were the cause of his unrest.

He did not want to be forced to select a queen. Far too long he'd ruled alone, answered to no one and liked it just fine that way. He did not require the assistance of a female.

Few men did.

Females tended to talk too much and think with their hearts, not their minds. Such was a luxury men could not afford. He shuddered to think what would come to be should females ever rule the realm. There would be nothing but talk, talk, talk.

He nearly groaned at the thought.

"A curse on the prophecy," he muttered,

making Sachin laugh. He looked to his friend. "They are wrong to put such stock in charms and magiks."

"At one point in your life, you too believed the seers to be true and wise."

He scoffed. "'Twas before I knew better."

"You are most difficult, my lord."

"I could have you beheaded," Kabril returned.

Sachin merely snorted. "You could try."

The people of his kingdom assumed their issues with conceiving were due to his reluctance to accept what they deemed to be destiny. Kabril wasn't a staunch believer in the gods or of prophecy as he should be, but it came from being the one forced to accept a wife he did not want. As their ruler, it was his sworn duty to do what was best for the kingdom, regardless how much it pained him.

"My lord," Sachin pressed, his reluctance

to let the subject rest putting Kabril's already taxed nerves on edge. The man would not cease his endless prattle about the subject no matter how much Kabril deemed he do so.

Kabril knew. He'd tried to decree it law not to speak of the ordeal.

Sachin simply ignored him.

As was the norm.

Taking a deep, calming breath, Kabril reminded himself of how proud he was, and should always be, of his people's customs and beliefs. Although he was less than pleased with the Oracle—whom they held in such high esteem—choosing a bride for him. According to the prophecies, the Oracle would select a woman fit to lead his people, and he was honor-bound to obey. It was also said the union would produce children, something their kind sorely lacked. Once heavily populated, his lands were no longer bursting with the sounds of children singing and playing. In truth, Kabril could scarcely recall when the sounds indicative of children stopped, but he knew it had been far too long.

War had claimed the lives of many of his people. Still others, while immortal to a degree, possessed the ability to pass on to the afterlife should they so choose. There came a time in many people's lives when they were ready to move on. It mattered not what the cause was—their population was low, as was morale. Riches only did so much to calm the people. They wanted families.

"Cursed Magaious," he spat, not caring if he took one of the Epopisdeus' names in vain.

Sachin clapped acrimoniously. "Bringing down the wrath of the bird gods will surely ease your burden, my lord. For if you curse one, they all rise to strike."

"You push me too far, old friend." Kabril

smoothed his fingertips along the wood of his throne, ignoring the internal nudge to free his temper.

"You do not push yourself far enough."

Kabril hated when Sachin was right.

Giving Sachin a daring look, Kabril let loose another curse upon the gods. He once again selected the god he knew Sachin honored weekly in hopes of provoking his friend. He was in the mood for a fight and Sachin was always a worthy adversary. The two often sparred until matins. Depending upon the day, Sachin would either continue the match or lay his sword down to go honor the gods. Kabril had long since given up his prayers to higher powers. "A pox on Magaious and those who follow him blindly."

Sachin merely tipped his head a little and released an exasperated sigh. "Remind me again which of us is older? You seem to be acting like a fledgling, my lord."

Arguing with Sachin would get him nowhere since it was clear Sachin was not going to take his bait. Damn him for being levelheaded. Kabril hungered for an argument, even a sparring match. Steel upon steel would settle the debate. For there was nothing more soothing than the clang of steel and the vibration up one's arm from a good strike and an equally as good counterstrike.

Sachin would obviously give in to neither. Kabril truly hated when his advisor was calm. It took all the fun out of a good fight. Kabril drummed his fingers on his armrests, trying to devise a plan for avoiding marriage.

Especially to a human female.

For more information about these titles and other bestselling Mandy M. Roth titles please

visit www.MandyRoth.com

The Impatient Lord by Michelle M. Pillow

Bestselling Dragon Shifter Romance

* * *

An unlucky bride…

Riona Grey lives life on her own terms, traveling wherever the next spaceship is flying and doing what she must in order to get by. When her luck turns sour, she finds herself on a bridal ship heading to a marriage ceremony. A planet full of dragon shifters seeking mates wasn't exactly what she had in mind as a final destination. Just when she thinks things couldn't possibly get worse, she wakes up months later in an isolation chamber with a sexy, hovering dragon shifter by her side telling her they're meant to be together...forever.

The impatient groom...

After years of failed marriage attempts at the Breeding Festivals, the gods finally revealed Lord Mirek's bride...a day too late.

Eager to have her, he defied tradition and laid claim. But it is a mistake to go against the gods and his new wife was the one to pay the price of his impatience.

Now almost a year later, his bride is finally waking from her deep sleep. With one look from her, he feels the eagerness to claim her overtaking him once more. Fearful she'll slip through his grasp once again, he's hesitant to anger the gods by taking her to his bed too soon. But, how can he resist the one thing that would make his life complete, especially when she looks at him with eyes of a seductress? This is one test he can't fail, and yet with one of her sweet kisses he knows he may already have lost.

The Impatient Lord (Dragon Lords) Excerpt

"What happened to you?" Alek eyed Mirek in concern. "Did you have to wrestle negotiate with the Syog again?"

"My wife." Mirek stopped his slow, ambling walk and leaned against the corridor wall. Not that he would complain, but Riona had taken to intimacy with a vivacious force he'd ever dreamed possible. "She's, ah, fully recovered now."

Alek quirked a brow. It took him a long moment to understand what was happening. His concern turned into hard, full laughter. He clutched his stomach and bent over, struggling to breathe.

"What's going on out here?" Bron appeared from the scroll room, holding a stack of yellowed parchments. He eyed his brothers curiously.

"Lady…learned…sex…balls," was about all of Alek's answer they could understand.

Mirek grimaced. He should have known better than to admit soreness to one of his brothers. Why hadn't he lied and said he'd been getting his privates kicked in a Syog ball racking negotiation? It would have been an easy lie. Those aliens were rough on the manhood, even if they used a semi-protective plate. No one would have questioned his claim. They would have still laughed at him, but they would have believed him.

"Mirek?" Bron asked in concern.

"Riona, ah— " Mirek began.

"He can't handle...his wife," Alek interrupted in merriment. "He's walking like this." Alek ambled around the hall like an old man with a cane, stumbling all the more in his fit of laughter.

Bron arched a brow and nodded his head. "Nicely done. We'll have another nephew to add to the family soon. Well done, brother."

"If she didn't break him," Alek inserted. "I always suspected you were a little soft,

Ambassador. All that flying in space and drinking lady wine with the aliens."

Mirek shoved Alek into a wall. It didn't stop the laughter as the man slid to the floor. "At least I don't smell like a ceffyl herd."

"I deserve that," Alek admitted, not bothering to stand as he grinned up at them. A change had come over him since his marriage. He was happier and smiled more. Whatever Kendall had done to her husband, she'd managed to tame the stubborn man.

"You're going to tell everyone, aren't you?" Mirek sighed, not really worried. His wife wanted him. That was a good thing. Actually, she wanted him…and wanted him…and wanted him…and—

"Oh, yeah," Alek nodded. "Everyone."

"Alek," Bron broke in. "Maybe we should keep this to ourselves. If my wife is any indication of how the women were raised, her sister will not like being talked about in such a way. She will consider it insulting."

Alek instantly agreed. "Of course, I didn't think of it like that. I would never gossip about my sisters if it made them uncomfortable."

"Thank you," Mirek mouthed. Bron nodded once.

"Have either of you seen the updated communications plans?" Bron asked, nodding at his armload. "We're having a hard time locating some of the buried mountain lines to see if they're salvageable. Aeron wants to get the construction plans finished before the baby arrives and keeps asking if they're lines or transmit boosters. I honestly have no idea how they work."

"Why don't you just grab a line on one side and pull?" Alek asked, shrugging. "See where it leads. If it doesn't lead anywhere, I'd say we have transmit boosters. I don't know what a transmit booster looks like, but we can send the boys out to look for one in the trees or wherever."

"Apparently checking the line that way will take longer. Aeron ordered a ground imager but it won't be here until after the baby comes. She is *very* focused on getting this done. Now." Bron looked at them hopefully, an almost desperate plea on his face as he wanted to please his pregnant wife. "So have you seen the updated plans?"

"Updated as in the ones from fifty years ago?" Mirek frowned. "Did we even have plans? I don't ever remember seeing them. I seem to remember Sper just making it work. He'd go out with tools and come back later with everything working again."

"Alek?" Bron prompted.

"No clue," Alek said. "I think Sper kept all the plans in his head. When he died, he took the information with him. Though, come to think of it, after he died the network stopped breaking down so much. I wonder what that man was doing?"

"Intergalactic transmissions," Mirek answered. Sper never married, never even tried to marry. He was a very rare exception to the Draig culture in that way. "Something he called moving, moodies, movies?"

"Blast!" Bron frowned. "That's what I was afraid of. Aeron is not going to be pleased. She is a very organized woman." To Mirek, he said, "She was always like that, but it's getting worse. At first, she just arranged clothing in the closet according to styles and color. But then I caught her trying to alphabetize your giant trade agreement reports in my office in the middle of the night."

"Wait until your bride starts hiding your favorite throwing knives," Alek said. "I wish

Kendall would merely reorganize reports."

A King's Ransom by Reagan Hawk

(pen name of Mandy M. Roth)

Book One in the Masters of Pleasure Series

On a quest to find his brother, King Kritan of Katarius on the planet of Panucia finds himself ambushed, beaten, tortured and then sold to fight in the arena games. The people of Tamonius—his rival kingdom—condone slavery, take public sex to new lows and try to turn a profit off anything they can. Nothing can change his hatred for everything Tamonius… That is, until he meets the most breathtakingly beautiful woman he's ever laid eyes upon. Surina of the House of Argyros, daughter to a powerful senator, stirs the beast within him, making it want to lay claim to her as badly as the man does.

Free or not, Kritan is a master of seduction, and has selected Surina as his newest prey. But this virginal beauty has secrets of her own—ones that change everything. And destiny just might have the last laugh.

Excerpt from A King's Ransom (Masters of Pleasure)

City of Vesta in the Kingdom of Tamonius on the Planet Panucia…

Kritan of Katarius walked through the streets of Vesta, a city known across the planet for its corruption and wickedness. He drew his black cloak around him more—to hide the sword at his side and the dagger in the top of his left boot. The clothing he wore was appropriate for the area, though nothing he'd normally want upon his body—the material was something a commoner would wear and not to his liking. He preferred trews to the tunic with a roped belt. He liked his boots, not the ones he wore now that were more of a sandal, leaving some of his foot exposed. He disliked, too, the ring that held his sword, preferring his sheath. He had not dared to bring his personal sword and shield. They were things that would give his origins—and his role—away.

It was important to blend. At least for now.

Cool wind from the north, from across the Ice Seas, blew past him. It was welcome against the heat of Tamonius's summer. Kritan preferred slightly cooler weather. While he could warm his body naturally by allowing his beast to rise, he could not cool it as easily.

His lip curled at the sight of three women standing, their breasts hanging out of the tops of their tunics. They were whores. His homeland, Katarius, was not without pleasures of the flesh, but they did not openly display their sexuality as the people of Tamonius did. While Katarius had whores, the guards there policed the streets better, making sure the women who charged were corralled into taverns or brothels, not left to wander the streets aimlessly for any and all to see. So far Kritan had lost count of the number of women he'd seen since entering the walls of Vesta who were selling their bodies for a few measly coins or even stale bread.

Such a state of things. And the Tamoni thought they were so superior to the six occupied countries on their home planet.

Kritan walked with his head up, moving with purpose, though he was not yet sure of where he needed to be. His informant had spoken of a tavern four roads within the gates of Vesta. As Kritan walked the length of the fourth row, he could count at least five taverns directly around him, each filthier than the last.

Unease settled over him. He had known this would be a fool's mission. One he should not have undertaken himself, but he'd had no choice. He had to find his brother. He had to make amends, and he would walk through the cesspool called Vesta a thousand times over if he thought it would give him a chance to make things right. Banishing Jaelyn all those years ago had been a mistake. One he'd lived with for nearly two decades. Lies and a woman—a woman Kritan had believed meant more to him than she did—had fostered an environment that left him speaking words he could not take back, and sending his brother far from home. So long had gone by with no word on his brother's whereabouts, that when a missive arrived telling a tall tale—one that spoke of Jaelyn not only being alive but in grave danger, so much so that his brother was suddenly on borrowed time, Kritan could not stop himself. He'd mounted a steed and set forth on a quest to find the man—to hell with the cost. Regardless that he had men to do such things for him. That, as King of Katarius, rushing alone into the kingdom of Tamonius was not simply reckless, it was suicide. This was his brother and he would right the wrong he'd committed long ago.

"You look like you like it rough," a whore said, cupping her unimpressive breasts as she wiggled for him. It was clear to see the woman had serviced many cocks in her days and life had not been kind to her.

Her friend and fellow whore slinked her arms over the woman's shoulders and flicked her tongue, as if being offered a threesome would create a more appealing sight for him to behold. Kritan was no stranger to threesomes, foursomes and more. But he would never soil himself with the likes of these women. All the face paint in the kingdom could not hide the signs of disease on their skin, and the reek of strong spirits they'd been drinking could not mask the fact they had not bathed in months.

Maybe more. Both looked heavily used and past their prime. Neither motivated his cock.

He had been too long between fucks and should have felt his beast stirring, wanting release. As a Katarian male shifter he was immune to the diseases that plagued the non-shifters—sexual or not. Though dirty whores never tempted him. He had certain standards, ones belonging to a king. There were many women who begged to be at his service within his castle, ready to ease his cock should he but click his fingers. All were screened by him before being granted such a coveted position. And sometimes, when he felt randy, he would sneak away to the buttery with a serving wench or two.

Regardless how long it had been since he'd fucked, his focus remained firm—find his brother.

Find Jaelyn.

Nothing else mattered.

To find out more about these books or to read other books from The Raven Books visit www.TheRavenBooks.com

CPSIA information can be obtained
at www.ICGtesting.com
Printed in the USA
LVOW08s2148120217
524067LV00003B/286/P